THE ISLAND WEDDING

Getaway Bay, Book 7

ELANA JOHNSON

ISBN-13: 978-1-63876-009-2

Chapter One

Wyatt Gardner sat in his police cruiser, watching person after person walk down the sidewalk in front of him. Most of them were women, and they were dressed nicely, with wedges and pumps and skirts, so he knew they were going to the September Sandy Singles event.

That was why he'd driven from the police station to the community center, too. He just couldn't quite get himself to get out of the car. Yet.

But he was going to get out. He was going to go in. He was going to put himself out there again. Try to find someone that he could spend the rest of his life with. He was only forty-four years old. He had a lot of life to live yet.

With Jennifer out of the house completely now, married and living her best life, Wyatt had plenty of time and money to move on. Plus, he really wanted to do the same thing his daughter had done. Find someone to love as completely as she had.

He'd been working for the Getaway Bay Police Department for twenty-three years now, and he was seriously thinking about hanging up his hat. Permanently.

But the thought of sitting around his house all day, nothing to do…he couldn't even imagine that, and that kept him getting up every morning, running along the beach, and going into the station.

"Going in," he said, as if he were letting his crew know at the station so they could send back-up if he didn't check in soon. He got out of the car and looked both ways down the sidewalk. But everyone would know where he was going and why he'd come the moment he stepped inside.

Wyatt held his head high and nodded to another man as he approached. He didn't know the guy, but most people in Getaway Bay knew Wyatt. So he nodded and stepped in line with him. "Can I go in with you?"

"Of course, Chief." The other guy gave him a smile, and they went through the marked door so other patrons of the community center who weren't attending the singles event could still use the facilities.

"What's your name?" he asked the man.

"Henry Bishop," he said.

"Nice to meet you, Henry." They met a line, and Wyatt slowed to join it. He wasn't particularly good with small talk, but he'd had plenty of practice over the years. "What do you do?"

"I'm a surfing instructor," he said. "Own a little hut in East Bay."

"Oh, that's great," Wyatt said. "I love surfing."

Henry smiled at him again, and a couple of women in front of them turned around. "I've used your surfing lessons," one of them said. "They were good."

"Yeah?" Henry asked. "Who was your instructor?"

"I can't remember." She twirled a lock of her dark hair around her ear. "Do you give lessons?"

"Of course, yeah," Henry said with a smile. "You didn't learn the first time?"

The brunette shrugged. "It's been a while, and I think I'm ready to get back in the water."

Wyatt was pretty sure her comment was some sort of euphemism he didn't understand, and he simply stood outside the trio as they continued to chat about surfing lessons and the best places to catch the biggest waves.

He entered last behind them, not catching either woman's name as they moved ahead of him. The scent of coconuts and suntan oil met his nose when he entered the room after logging his name with the clerk standing at the door.

This singles event was a free couple of hours on a Friday night, and with summer in full swing, Wyatt had decided now was a great time to branch out of his usual find-a-date tactics. That honestly wasn't hard, because he currently had no tactics to find a date. Most of the women he came in contact with were under arrest or employees. The department didn't have rules against relationships among co-workers, as long as all the proper paperwork was filed. But Wyatt had never wanted to be with a fellow cop.

Piper had been his complete opposite in every way, and he'd loved her with everything in him. When she'd died, a piece of Wyatt had died too.

For a while there, he'd thought it was the most important part of himself. But through his grief counseling, and with the passage of time, he'd learned that he still had the capacity to love. He'd seen friends move past difficult divorces, as well as the loss of loved ones. One of his good friends from their grief meetings had just gotten married, and Wyatt had been spurred by Cal's example to find his own date.

Tonight, he told himself as he surveyed the room. The cop inside him couldn't help checking for all the exits and looking around for a safe place to hide should something happen. He estimated the number of people in the room to be about one hundred, and the vast majority of them were women.

Wyatt supposed he should be happy about that, but all he felt was pressure. A lot of pressure. He could get a phone number tonight from someone who wasn't really that interested in him. She might only talk to him, because there weren't that many other men to choose from.

He took a deep breath, stepped over to the refreshment table, which was smartly placed by the entrance, and grabbed a plastic cup of punch. With something to occupy his attention, he took a drink and surveyed the groups of women closest to him. He'd been under the impression there would be structured activities during the Sandy Singles event, but if so, they hadn't started yet.

He'd taken one step when someone came over the microphone. "All right, everyone. We're about to start our first speed-dating activity. I need all women on the left side of the room. All the men on the right. That's right. Women on the left. Men on the right."

Wyatt followed the directions, and he'd been right. Only about twenty-five percent of the attendees were men, and he hoped the organizer of these activities knew what to do with the extra women.

"We're going to divide the women into three groups," the woman at the mic said. "Men, I hope you have a drink nearby and are ready to chat." She beamed at the right side of the room, and Wyatt swallowed his nerves.

He was good at talking to strangers. He could make someone he suspected of heinous crimes talk to him, trust him, connect with him. A woman was somehow harder, but he pushed his nerves away.

He didn't want to live the next thirty years alone. Or even another one.

So he put a smile on his face, took the seat he was given, and prepared himself to talk to people for the next couple of hours.

A woman with dirty blonde hair sat in front of him, her blue eyes sparkling like sunlight off the ocean. Her hair was all piled up on top of her head like she'd walked into the event from off the beach, and Wyatt smiled at her.

Not his type.

But he could be nice. "I'm Wyatt Gardner," he said, extending his hand.

"Everyone knows who you are," she said with a smile. She put her hand in his and cocked her head. "I'm Bridgette Baker."

"Nice to meet you," he said, thinking he was a better liar than he'd like to be. The small talk was small with Bridgette, and when the bell rang, the women got up and moved down a seat. Wyatt looked to his right, realizing he had a very long night ahead of him.

After five rounds of speed-dating, he'd taken two slips of paper from women he would not be calling, and he got to his feet when the organizer said, "Five-minute break, and then we'll start with the second group of women."

Yeah, Wyatt wouldn't be. He'd thought this Sandy Singles even was a good idea, and he was willing to admit it when he was wrong.

He headed for the door, not caring how many people saw him. The whole island knew about Piper's death, and they'd just assume he was still too broken up over her death to date. Or they'd speculate that he'd gotten an emergency call. In fact, he pulled out his phone and looked at it, tapping as if sending a text to someone very important.

In truth, the only place he needed to be was on his

couch, a really great fish taco in his hands, and the television lulling him to sleep.

Pathetic, maybe. But right now, Wyatt was okay with that.

In his peripheral vision, he caught sight of someone directly in front of him. Someone he was about to run into. He looked up at the same time he collided with the woman, who obviously hadn't been watching where she was going either.

"Oof," she said, and to Wyatt's great horror, she fell backward. Her eyes widened, and she cried out as she fell in super-slow motion. Wyatt tried to reach for her, but she flailed out of his reach. Way out of his reach, because he'd just bowled over Deirdre Bernard.

She hit the ground, and everything that had slowed down raced forward again. "Deirdre," Wyatt said, his voice mostly air. He hurried over to her and knelt down. "I'm so sorry." He didn't quite know where to put his hands.

His brain screamed at him to do something helpful. *Apologize. Say you're ready.*

He just hovered above Deirdre, his memories streaming through him now. Memories of the relationship they'd tried. The things she'd said to him when they'd broken up. All of those were true, and Deirdre deserved some credit for Wyatt's reappearance at the grief meetings on the island.

Their eyes met, and Wyatt put his hands at his sides. "Are you okay?"

"I'm okay," she said, and Wyatt wanted to smooth her hair, tuck the errant locks behind her ear, and apologize for not being ready last time.

Could there be a *this* time?

"Let me help you," he said, giving her his hand and helping her stand up. "Sorry, I wasn't watching where I was going."

"I wasn't either." She smoothed down her blouse and looked at Wyatt fully again. "Look at us, running into each other. Literally." Deirdre smiled, and Wyatt remembered how beautiful she was when she did. His heartbeat accelerated, and he definitely wanted a second chance with this woman.

"What are you doing right now?" he asked boldly.

"Right this second?"

"Yeah."

She looked over her shoulder toward the room he'd just exited. "Well, there's this singles event a couple of my girlfriends came to. I've been waiting in the car, and —" She gave a light laugh. "I finally decided to come in."

"I was just headed out, and I'm starving. Do you want to grab some dinner?"

"With you?"

"Yes," Wyatt said, hoping she wouldn't say no. How humiliating would that be?

Deirdre narrowed her eyes slightly and seemed to peer directly into his soul. "Wyatt, you're a great man. But I don't…it didn't work last time, and I don't think it's going to work this time." She patted his bicep as she stepped around him.

Wyatt turned, speechless, and watched her enter the Sandy Singles event room.

What a disaster. Swallowing back his embarrassment, Wyatt held his head as high as he could as he walked out of the community center and back to his cruiser.

There weren't enough fish tacos on the planet to erase this night from his memory.

Chapter Two

Deirdre Bernard refused to put her name on the roster of people who'd come to the September Sandy Singles event at the community center. The last thing she needed was a ton of emails clogging her inbox. She didn't need to know about the scrapbooking nights or the sewing club or another one of these disastrous events.

How she'd allowed Meg to talk her into coming, she still wasn't sure. She didn't pick up a drink and instead, chose a spot in the corner behind the refreshment table. A bell rang, and the women sitting at the table got up and moved one spot to the right.

Yeah, no thanks, Deirdre thought. She could admit there was something missing in her life, but that didn't mean the hole was man-shaped. Her entire life had crumbled in the past couple of years, and she'd been rebuilding it one brick at a time.

New job. New city. New life. She'd tried a new man, but Wyatt hadn't been ready. And if Deirdre was being completely truthful, she hadn't been either, though her divorce was five years old.

Her mind immediately moved to Emma, the sixteen-year-old daughter she'd left on the north side of the island with her father and Deirdre's ex-husband. When her daughter had made that choice, everything in Deirdre's life had exploded.

Maybe she did need whatever was in those plastic cups on the table.

"All right," a woman said into the microphone. "Our next activity is called Blind Date. I need everyone back on their sides." The men and women divided themselves onto different sides of the room, and Deirdre couldn't believe they'd subjected themselves to this activity. It was humiliating, and she felt bad for them.

At that moment, she realized why Wyatt had left, and she wanted to follow him right out the door. So she did. Deirdre could run down the beach and get a pork pot sticker and be back before Meg even knew she'd gone. Her stomach grumbled, because her friend had promised her dinner after this insane dating spectacle. But Meg would probably find a guy to take to dinner, and they both knew it.

Deirdre went back out the door she'd gone in, the air easier to breathe the moment she left the dating game behind. Why would anyone subject themselves to a game like that? She made a mental note to ask Meg what she found so appealing about the Sandy Singles events.

She didn't want to judge though. She knew everyone was different, and while a Sandy Singles event was at the bottom of her list to attend, clearly someone enjoyed it. The Getaway Bay Community Center put on an event every single month. After driving over to her favorite bistro, she stalled at the sight of the long line stretching out the door and down the sidewalk.

"Dang," she muttered to herself. No pot stickers tonight. She thought of a taco stand over in Getaway Bay that had super-fast service, and she headed toward the beach. There were a lot of people here too, because a September evening on the beach was simply spectacular. The palm trees. The breeze off the bay. The clear blue sky, fading to gold and crimson.

People milled about, but the line to order at the stand wasn't long, and Deirdre joined it. A few minutes later, she put in her order for three fish tacos, and someone said, "If I'd known you liked those, I would've brought you some."

She turned to find Wyatt standing there. He crumpled up his taco papers and tossed them in the trashcan. He gave her a devilish smile that made her body light up, and then he tipped an imaginary hat at her. "Good to see you, Deirdre."

With that, he walked away, leaving Deirdre wishing she'd said yes to his dinner invitation. She might have had she known his idea of a fun, delicious evening was on this beach, with these tacos.

Might have? she thought. She definitely would have, though the tacos weren't the deciding factor. Wyatt Gardner was very good-looking, and he didn't even seem to know it.

Why had she said no earlier?

People looked at him everywhere he went, and Deirdre hadn't minded being on his arm for the month they dated. He was mature, and that went a long way for her.

She watched him leave the beach and climb behind the wheel of his police cruiser. She had his number. She could call him.

"Don't get too excited," she muttered to herself. She'd text. Deirdre only called her brides or a vendor to make sure everything was set for the high-end weddings she planned at Your Tidal Forever.

The man leaning out of the taco shack called her name, and Deirdre collected her tacos. She found a patch of sand and watched the sun finish setting into the ocean, a spicy fish taco the perfect complement to her evening.

She lost herself in thoughts of Wyatt–until her phone rang and Meg's name sat on the screen.

"Shoot," she muttered, fumbling the phone as she realized she'd been gone from the community center for far too long. She got the call open, finally. "Hey," she said brightly.

"Where are you?" Meg demanded. "And do *not* tell me you went to get those pot stickers from Bora Bora's."

Thankfully, Deirdre couldn't tell her that, and she simply said, "I'll be there in five minutes."

———

"No, I can't hold," she said the next day. She didn't normally work weekends, but she had a wedding in a week, and she'd gotten a message at closing time yesterday that the vines she'd ordered would not be delivered in time.

"I'm sorry," she said, making her voice a little sweeter. "I'm just returning Madison's call, and I really need to talk to her as soon as possible."

"She's not in today," the girl on the other end of the line said.

"I know that," Deirdre said. "Who else can I talk to about an order that I've had in for three months?"

"Please hold," the girl said, not asking this time. Deirdre couldn't protest, because she'd literally just asked to talk to someone who could help her. Disgusting elevator music came through the line, and she pushed the speaker button so she didn't have to hold the device to her ear the whole time.

She looked at the files on her at-home desk, but she didn't have anything else to do for this wedding. All the last-minute checks had been done this week, and they'd all come through—except for these vines.

The music cut off, and Deirdre picked up the phone, expecting to hear the voice of someone who could help her. Instead the screen went black. "Did she hang up on me?"

The call had definitely ended, and Deirdre's frustration rose through the roof as she practically stabbed her device to get the phone dialing again.

"Jungle Plants," the same girl said.

"Yes, hello," Deirdre said, a definite bite in her voice. "My name is Deirdre Bernard. I'm a wedding planner at Your Tidal Forever, and I had a three-month order that I was told wouldn't be able to be fulfilled. I need to talk to someone about this order and what can be done about it. I have a bride expecting the ten-foot vines that you suddenly can't deliver."

"Did Julie not pick up?"

"No," Deirdre said. "Julie did not pick up. Does Julie have a direct line?"

"I'll transfer you. Please hold."

"No—" Deirdre cut off as the sleepy music started again. A sigh came out of her mouth as she put the phone back on speaker.

A text came in over the top of the call, and she caught Meg's name. A blip of fear moved through her, because Meg had lectured her the whole way home about "getting out there" and that she'd seen her talking to Wyatt. How that was even possible, Deirdre didn't know. But Meg taught third grade, and it was possible she had eyes in the back of her head, underneath all that dark hair.

Deirdre had said she wanted to hear all about the speed-dating, and if Meg had met someone worth dating, but a woman chirped, "This is Julie," before Deirdre could pick up her phone.

"Yes, hi, Julie. I have an order that's been in for three months, and I got a call yesterday that it wouldn't be fulfilled. I need those vines, and I'm wondering if there's anything you can do for me."

Silence came through the line, and Deirdre checked to make sure she hadn't been hung up on again. The timer was still ticking at the top of the screen. Julie just wasn't saying anything.

"Hello?" Deirdre asked.

"I'm sorry," Julie said. "You need to talk to our administration office, and they're not in on the weekends."

"I know," Deirdre said. "I already explained that to the girl who answered the phone. She said you could help me."

"Uh, I can't even access the computer system on the weekends."

Deirdre blinked, and her vision went red for a moment. "Thank you." She hung up this time, because she didn't need to cause a scene. Hope and Shannon had been very clear about that. Things happened sometimes. Deirdre was to be professional even when things weren't going her way.

She sank into her office chair and opened Meg's text. Rumors flying at the police station this morning. You sure you didn't go out with Wyatt?

A vision of Wyatt entered Deirdre's mind, but she didn't want to mention that yes, he'd been at the taco stand. *I went and got tacos*, she tapped out. *Did you meet anyone noteworthy?*

There were hardly any men there, Meg responded. *It was lame.*

Deirdre could've told her that the dating event would be quite lame, but she didn't need to rub it in. *Sorry.*

What are you doing today?

Deirdre looked at the folder on her desk, a sigh moving through her whole body. *Nothing. Thinking about going to a movie or something.*

As soon as Deirdre sent the text, she realized she didn't want to leave the house. *Maybe I'll just make a fruit salad and lounge on my couch.*

Meg couldn't stand to hold still for longer than five seconds, so lounging on the couch wouldn't be in her wheelhouse. *Boring*, she sent with a smiley face emoji. *I'm taking Father John to the beach. We're going paddle boarding. You should come.*

And watch you and your dog paddle board? No thanks.

Deirdre liked Meg, and they'd started at Your Tidal Forever within a week of each other. They'd relied on each other quite a lot as they learned the ropes of the company, but Deirdre didn't get super close to people very quickly.

Then she had to tell them things about her life she

didn't want anyone to know. Or rather, she didn't mind if people knew about her life before Getaway Bay, but she only wanted people to know who she explicitly trusted.

All right, Meg said. *Be that way. See you Monday.*

Deirdre sent a thumbs-up and turned back to her house. "Well, what should we do today?" She hadn't put out any cat food for the strays who frequented this street, so she took a few minutes to do that.

She wanted to text Emma and find out how school was going, but she didn't need to be accused of being overbearing or controlling. Again. Her chest tightened, and she opted to simply type out a quick note.

Hope school was awesome this week. I love you.

She would not send the message to her daughter, though. Contact with her daughter was prohibited. Deirdre could talk to Dalton, and she sometimes asked about Emma, though that could technically be against the rules of her order too.

But she needed to know Emma was still alive, and the only way Deirdre knew that was because Dalton said she was.

Deirdre wasn't sure how she'd come out the bad guy with Emma, not when she'd done everything to protect her daughter from Dalton's behavior. But of course, Emma didn't know what Deirdre had done to make her childhood as normal as possible. What she'd shielded her from. What sacrifices she'd made for her daughter, some at a great personal loss for her.

She hadn't given up the only communication she had

with her daughter easily, but in the end, she *had* given it up. Emma hadn't responded to her texts for a month before Deirdre had been forced to stop talking to her daughter, but not a day went by that Deirdre didn't think about Emma and wish things were different.

She wondered what Wyatt did on the weekends, since they'd only had a few together. He'd worked a couple of them, and Deirdre had the sudden urge to steal something. Then maybe she'd get to see him again without being too obvious.

Scratch that, she thought. Getting arrested just to see the Chief of Police was definitely too obvious. So how did she get Wyatt's attention…again?

Chapter Three

W yatt sat on his deck, a glass of lemonade beside him that would take him an hour to finish. He loved the first, very cold sip, and he loved the last, almost warm one too. He liked watching the waves roll ashore on the beach about a mile away, but he didn't have to be around people to do it.

He spent so much time around people, and sometimes he really needed a day of no talking. Now that Jennifer was married and off the island, Wyatt could go hours without speaking to someone.

Turned out, the silence wasn't as wonderful as he'd imagined it might be. He reached down and stroked Tigger, the German shepherd mix he'd found tangled in a buoy line a few years ago. No collar. He'd put out the word about the lost dog through every channel he had in Getaway Bay, but no one had come forward to claim the dog.

And Christine had just passed away, and Wyatt had needed a new companion. He loved Tigger with everything in him, and the dog sure did seem to like him too. He took him to work, to the grocery store, everywhere the dog could go and not have to wait in the hot car.

"She told me no, Tig," he said to the dog, still fixated on Deirdre's rejection of him from the previous night. He'd thought about calling her and asking her to join him for tacos that night, but he still had some pride when it came to the woman.

He'd messed things up with them last time, and she'd obviously moved past him. They'd only gone out for a month, and he had been severely unavailable during that time. He couldn't blame her for patting his chest and saying, "Wyatt, this isn't working. I don't think you're ready."

She'd been kind, and Wyatt had always been attracted to her physically and emotionally. She had a heart of gold, and there was so much more about her he wanted to know.

His phone bleeped out a sound that indicated his sergeant had messaged. Wyatt didn't want to look at the text, but he couldn't ignore it for very long. He took another sip of lemonade and drew in a long, deep breath. Then he picked up the phone.

Cam Locke was a good man. He ran a tight ship when he was in charge, and he'd be a good Chief when Wyatt retired.

How was the Sandy Singles event?

Wyatt rolled his eyes. He couldn't believe he'd broken his tranquil afternoon to read a text like that. His stomach growled for more than lemonade, and while he still had his phone in his hand, he saw that the food delivery app had Nuts About Dough listed as open. While it wasn't breakfast time anymore, the pastry shop did stay open later on weekends, and a Morning Sunrise would hit the spot about now.

Sausage patty, over-easy egg, delicious mayo mixed with relish, all on a doughnut for a bun. And it would show up at his house in less than twenty-five minutes.

Satisfied with his purchase, he set his phone back on the table and faced the water again. "Then we'll go chase a ball, okay?"

Tigger didn't answer, but Wyatt knew the dog would perk right up the moment the tennis ball came out. The dog would literally do anything to find it, and Wyatt did love watching him dig in the sand until Tigger found his mark. With the proper training, he could be a good rescue or drug dog, but he hadn't gotten started with the training early enough in his life.

His breakfast sandwich arrived, and Wyatt took his time eating it, the same way he savored his lemonade. Really, he was buying time until he had to leave the shade of his deck and take the dog to the beach. But he'd be happier if he did, because then Tigger would sleep for a bit that evening.

Not that Wyatt had anything to do that night. Maybe

more tacos. A shaved ice. Alone. He wondered if he would always be alone.

Maybe his heart could stand the thought of another rejection if the possibility of not being alone was the reward.

Maybe.

———

MONDAY MORNING, WYATT WALKED INTO THE POLICE station, the activity there a little too high, even for a Monday morning. "Morning, Norma," he said to his secretary, and she immediately shot to her feet.

"Sir, there's a woman in your office."

"Oh?" He picked up his mail and looked at Norma. "Good visit or bad?"

"That depends on the woman, doesn't it?" She grinned, and Wyatt decided that certainly couldn't mean he had an angry patron in his office, though Norma usually kept them away fairly easily.

"Well, who is it?" He glanced toward his office door, but it was closed. "And thanks for telling everyone about the Sandy Singles event."

"What?" She pressed one hand to her chest in mock horror. "I didn't tell anyone anything."

"Mm hm," he said, disinterested in his mail but still looking at it like he cared. "Right. That's why Cam texted me over the weekend."

"Maybe he was there."

"He wasn't."

"How did it go?"

Wyatt looked up and met Norma's eye. "Never let me go to one of those again."

"Maybe Cam just happened to see it on your calendar," Norma said, a smile blooming across her face. "And you know, my sister—"

"Nope," Wyatt said, cutting her off quickly. "I can get my own dates." He'd told Cal Lewiston, a friend from his grief meetings, the same thing. So the Sandy Singles event hadn't worked out. There were other ways to meet women. In fact, he had one waiting for him in his office right now.

As if summoned by his thoughts, the office door opened, drawing his attention there. "Deirdre?" He cut a glance at Norma. "Why didn't you say it was Deirdre?" He barely hissed the words out of the corner of his mouth as he dropped his mail back on Norma's desk and stepped toward his office.

Deirdre looked okay. She hadn't been crying. But why was she here? "Are you okay? What's going on?"

She kept her gaze past him, clearly watching Norma. Smart, as his secretary had the hearing of an eagle. Or a deer. A dog. Whichever animal had really good hearing, that was Norma.

He took Deirdre by the elbow and nudged her into his office. His fingers tingled though he was forty-four years old. When the door clicked closed behind him, he asked again, "What are you doing here?"

"How was your weekend, Chief?"

She wanted to talk about his weekend? Wyatt watched her with a wary eye, wondering what kind of game this was. The Deirdre Bernard he knew didn't play games. "Truthfully? It was dull. Boring. The highlight was when my dog rolled in the mud and I got to hose him down."

Deirdre's eyes sparkled like light blue diamonds. Like sunlight glinting off the waves he loved to watch. A laugh burst from her mouth, and she covered it with her hand. "Wow, that was the highlight?"

"Well, I didn't find a date on Friday night, so yes. That was the highlight. Oh, but me and the delivery guys from FoodNow are getting tight."

"You use FoodNow?"

"I love FoodNow," he said. "It's a game-changer for me. You haven't used it?"

"I prefer to cook at home," she said coolly.

Wyatt rounded his desk and sat down, probably a dozen things on his to-do list for the day. He'd know as soon as he powered on his computer, which he made no move to do. "So, Miss Bernard. What can I do for you?"

She cleared her throat and approached the desk, sitting in the chair opposite him. "I'm in trouble."

"Oh?" His eyebrows went up, but his gaze remained steady.

"Yeah."

"I know you're going to be late for work," he said. "Is that the kind of trouble you're talking about?"

"No." Those eyes positively glittered at him, and Wyatt realized with a start that she was flirting with him. *Flirting.* With *him.*

"Is this going to be a guessing game?" he asked.

"Yes."

"All right." He exhaled. "You're out of almond milk, and you don't have time to go to the store."

She shook her head.

"You got another cat."

"I don't actually own any cats, I'll have you know."

"Mm, interesting." Wyatt enjoyed this conversation, but he honestly had no idea what Deirdre needed from him. "Why don't you just tell me what kind of trouble you're in?"

"I'd really like some of those pork pot stickers for dinner tonight, but I hate going alone."

He blinked rapidly then, not caring that he'd given away his whole hand. "The pork pot stickers from Bora Bora?"

"That would be the place."

"I can see why that's a problem," he said. "I wouldn't call it trouble, but—semantics." He shrugged. "The lines have gotten long there, because the secret of the pork pot sticker seems to have spread far and wide on the island." He picked up his phone and turned it over in his hand. Over and over.

"Yeah," she said. "A real conundrum."

He swiped and tapped and turned the phone toward her. "We could just order from FoodNow.

Thirty minutes later, we have pork pot stickers at our disposal."

"Wyatt Gardner, are you asking me to come over and eat dinner with you tonight?"

Wyatt chuckled and shook his head. "Oh, no, I'm not doing that. I did that two nights ago, and I got put in my place." Two could play her flirting game, though she was definitely better at it than he was.

"What if I asked you to come over to *my* place and we could eat dinner together tonight?"

Wyatt considered her, sure he was about to open his chest and invite her to cut out his heart. "Well, then, I guess you've got yourself a date. I hear those FoodNow delivery guys are mostly single."

Chapter Four

Deirdre stared at Wyatt, who stared right back. "I'm not going out with one of the delivery guys," she said evenly. "A lot of them are women."

Wyatt leaned back in his chair and continued to watch her. Deirdre could see the intelligence in his eyes, and it actually made her as uncomfortable as it appealed to her.

"Okay," she said. "I am going to be late for work." She knocked a couple of times on his desk. "Good talk."

Deirdre couldn't believe she'd waited in his office for twenty minutes to ask him out, only to have him suggest she order in and ask the delivery driver out.

Humiliation filled her, and she thought about driving around the island to the north shore so Emma would report her for breaking the restraining order. Then she'd get arrested, and then Wyatt would have to pay attention to her.

Don't be ridiculous, she told herself as she approached Norma's desk. The woman had eyes like a hawk, and she'd hooked into Deirdre the moment she'd left Wyatt's office. "Oh, dear," she said. "He said no, didn't he?"

"Kind of?" Deirdre guessed. "It's fine, Norma. Thanks for letting me wait in his office." She'd been tempted to look through the files on his desk or jiggle his mouse to wake up his computer. She'd minded her manners, though, and she hadn't touched anything.

His face had lit up when he'd first seen her, but she'd underestimated the level of his hurt from her rejection a couple of nights ago. But she thought maybe if she showed up and asked him out, he'd forgive her.

She didn't know Wyatt Gardner as well as she thought, obviously. She walked through the maze of hallways that led to the parking lot, the sun already heating the day past comfortable. Deirdre didn't care. Your Tidal Forever had great air conditioning, and once she got to the office, she'd be fine.

She needed to call Jungle Plants the moment she got in, and then she'd need to powwow with Charlotte, Lisa, and Hope to figure out what to do about the vines they wouldn't have for the wedding that weekend.

She'd just reached her car when she heard someone call her name. Wyatt. Deirdre pressed her eyes closed before turning back to him. He walked toward her, his tall frame and wide shoulders calling to everything female inside her.

"I'm sorry," he said. "Is the dinner invitation still open?"

"Yes."

"I'd love to go to dinner with you."

"I can cook at my place."

"Sounds nice."

"Six?"

"I'll be there."

Deirdre nodded, determined not to tuck her hair behind her ear until the handsome Chief of Police walked away from her. He fell back a step but didn't turn around. Then another, a smile spreading across his face.

"Same house over on Parrot Street?" he asked.

"Yes."

He saluted her and finally turned around. Deirdre tucked her blonde hair behind her ear and sighed, suddenly not caring about the heat. She didn't want to play games with Wyatt, and it seemed like he didn't either.

She got behind the wheel of her car and turned the key in the ignition. The air conditioning blew, and she breathed in the cold air, finally allowing herself to smile. She'd gotten a date with the Chief of Police.

"You did it," she whispered to herself as she pulled out of the parking space and aimed her car toward Your Tidal Forever. When she got to work, she went into her office and put her purse in the closet right behind the door. Before she sat down and got to work, she left the office and went to the one immediately next door.

"Meg," she said, excitement building inside her. "You'll never guess what I did this morning."

Her friend looked up from her tablet, where she had a couple of sketches open for dresses.

"Oh, are those the bridesmaids dresses for the Carrolle wedding?"

"Yes." Meg turned the tablet so Deirdre could see it. "Aren't they great? Ash sent them over, but she thinks there's something missing."

Deirdre put Wyatt in the back of her mind for a moment. In another life, on the other side of the island, she'd known how to sew. In fact, in the early day of her marriage, she'd worked as a seamstress to bring in more money.

"I agree," she said slowly. "Has she thought about putting a bow in the back? That's coming back into trend these days. Huge bow, in a contrasting color."

Meg cocked her head at the tablet. "I'll text her." She swiped away from the sketches and opened her email. "What's going on with you this morning?"

"I got a date."

Meg abandoned the tablet completely. "Shut the front door. Tell me what happened."

"You were right about me running into Wyatt on Friday," she said. "And he asked me out, but I said no."

"You said no?" Meg shook her head. "Sometimes I really don't understand you."

Deirdre barely understood herself, and she was thirty-nine years old. "Anyway," she said pointedly. "I stopped by the police station this morning on my way in, and *I* asked *him* out."

Deirdre didn't need to go into how he'd said no at first, though him chasing her down in the parking lot was kind of romantic.

But Deirdre knew a relationship needed more than romance to work, and she'd often thought she didn't have all that many romantic bones in her body anyway.

"And he's coming over tonight for dinner."

"You're cooking?" Meg's eyebrows shot sky high. "Wow, that's brave."

"Why is that brave?" Deirdre sat down and crossed her legs.

Meg glanced toward the door, and Deirdre remembered she'd come in late already. She didn't want to upset Hope, but she also really wanted to get her head in the right place when it came to Wyatt. She could easily say she was talking to Meg about the vines.

"Before you say," she said. "Remind me that we need to talk about the vines for the wedding this weekend."

"Okay—what? The vines?"

"After," Deirdre said. "Why is it brave of me to have him to my place for dinner?"

"Because," Meg said matter-of-factly. "Then he's there, in your space. And you can't just be like, *I have to get up early. Let's go. Thanks for dinner*, like you can at a restaurant. What if he won't leave?"

"He has to get up early for work too," Deirdre said.

"Your funeral," Meg said, but Deirdre thought if she could taste her coconut shrimp and seafood risotto, Meg would change her tune. "Now, what's going on with the vines?"

Before Deirdre could tell her, her speakerphone beeped. "Meg," Sunny said. "Your nine o'clock is here." She sounded chipper and happy to be in on Monday morning, the same as always. "And she brought her mother," she added in a whisper. "Shall I send them back?"

"I'll come out to get them," Meg said. "Thanks, Sunny." She got up from behind her desk.

"Is this the La Costa wedding?"

"Yes." Meg sighed. "And let me tell you, just because they're Hawaiian royalty does not mean they know how to make a decision."

"Hawaiian royalty?"

"Oh, totally." Meg nodded as her heels clicked against the floor. "The mother is like the queen or priestess or whatever of their tribe. She scares me a little." She flashed Deirdre a smile and then turned back to her fully. "Oh, and I'm expecting a call tonight after your little dinner. Unless, of course, it's past ten. Then don't call. I need my beauty rest." With that, Meg was gone, leaving Deirdre to figure out why having Wyatt over for dinner would be like her funeral.

She hurried out of the office and into her own,

because she didn't need to be there when the Hawaiian royalty showed up.

She couldn't solve the vine problem, even with Hope and Charlotte on her side, and she made a difficult phone call to the bride to explain the vines. In the end, they decided to go with false ones, and Deirdre spent the afternoon at the local craft store trying to find the right thing.

Six o'clock approached as she zipped into the grocery store to buy a few key ingredients for dinner, including the coconut and the shrimp. She barely arrived home before six, but she didn't see Wyatt's police cruiser in her driveway. The tropical palm trees bordered both sides of the dirt road that led up to her house, and she felt secluded from the rest of the island, though she was only sixty seconds up Parrot Road and into the rain forest on the island.

She loved the sound of birds calling to each other in the trees, and the hint of wind she got off the ocean, only a couple of blocks away.

She set about starting the seafood risotto, because it would take the longest. Frying shrimp took only a few minutes, and Deirdre knew Wyatt loved seafood.

Mixing and measuring, Deirdre got the risotto going. As it bubbled away, she washed the shrimp and made the quick coconut breading. With a pan of oil heating next to her heavy saucepan where the risotto now needed more water, Deirdre returned her attention to the risotto.

So absorbed in the food prep as she as, Deirdre didn't

even realize what time it was until the risotto was plump and almost finished. Which meant thirty minutes had passed.

And Wyatt hadn't shown up yet.

Alarm pulled through Deirdre, and she actually turned and looked at the front door. He'd knock any moment now.... Any moment....

Chapter Five

Wyatt's frustration had reached its limit an hour ago, but he couldn't leave the scene of the accident. It felt like the world and everything in it was conspiring against him and Deirdre, who'd expected him for dinner a half an hour ago.

"Excuse me," he said to his sergeant, and Wyatt stepped away from the witnesses who couldn't seem to get their story straight. He had his doubts about whether they'd seen anything at this point, and he wasn't sure why Noel wanted to keep questioning them.

I'm not going to make it, he typed out. *I'm so sorry. Turn on the news and you'll know why.*

"Chief?"

He tapped *send* quickly and turned back to one of his officers. "Yep." He moved over to Sandi, who was crouched down in front of a bullet casing. "What have you got?"

"Why do you think this is here?" She indicated the casing. "Does it look new, or like it could've been here for a while?"

"Bag it anyway," Wyatt said, looking up at the office complex. Had there been a shooting here too? Or just a reckless driver who'd rammed straight through the wall?

He really liked putting together the pieces of a puzzle, and that was all a crime scene was. The car had missed the benches and fountain in front of the building, so it had hit at an angle, almost to the front entrance, but not quite.

Had that been planned?

The driver had gotten out of the car on his own volition, and the paramedics who'd arrived first had him strapped to a gurney in the back of the bus already. No one had questioned him yet, as his officers and several other teams of paramedics were still assessing all those who'd come pouring out of the building, or who'd been standing in the outside courtyard when the car had come careening off the street.

"Sandi," he said. "Spread the word to get everyone asking if anyone heard any gunshots."

"Yes, sir." She supervised the collection of the casing and then lifted her radio from her shoulder. Wyatt heard her voice come through his earpiece, and several officers looked his way.

He folded his arms, his silent affirmation that he wanted them to be sure to ask everyone about a gunshot or what they might have heard.

Part of him longed for his younger days when he was the one out questioning the witnesses, gathering the information he'd take to the staff meetings, the roundtables, the discussions with his superiors.

Problem was, now he was the superior, and all of his men and women would report to him. He'd assign a team of detectives to this case, and they'd take everything from there. But the initial gathering of information and actual forensic evidence was the most crucial stage of a new case.

He'd known when the call came in that he wouldn't make it to dinner with Deirdre, but he hadn't texted. His hope had gotten the best of him again.

His phone rang, and his heart leapt. But it was only Prudence Jorgenson, the woman who lived next-door to him. "Oh, no," he muttered under his breath. Tigger had probably been barking, and Pru wasn't happy about it. He hated bothering the older woman, and Wyatt would need to take her a box of her favorite pastries from Nuts About Dough and make sure he mowed her lawn on time.

"Mrs. Jorgenson," he said. "I'm sorry about Tigger. Has he been bothering you?"

"I heard him barking," she said, and she didn't seem upset. "So I went next door and got him. He's in my backyard, chasing squirrels."

"Pru," Wyatt said, smiling. "You didn't need to do that." And she could've broken a hip even though the distance between their houses was small.

"I've seen you on the news," she said. "It's no problem. He can stay the night if you're done late."

"And by late, you mean after eight."

"That's right, sonny," she said. "I don't open the door after dark."

Wyatt chuckled even as someone else called, "Chief."

"I need to go, Pru. Thanks for grabbing Tigger." He hung up before the woman could say anything else, already moving toward Noel. He and Tom would be the best choices for the detectives on this case, and Wyatt would check their workload when he got back to the office.

"Yeah," he said when he arrived.

"Mister Christopher says he heard a gunshot." He nodded to the man who'd first said he was sitting on the fountain wall. Then a bench. Then he'd been inside. Wyatt didn't believe a word he said.

"Oh?" He turned toward the dark-haired man. In Wyatt's expert opinion, the man certainly hadn't been inside the office building. This place housed a tech firm and a private physical therapy unit.

This guy wore a pair of basketball shorts and a tank top with a giant wolf head peering out at everyone. He wasn't injured, and he wasn't dressed like anyone from the technology firm. They all wore khakis and button-up shirts or stylish polos, and loafers.

More likely, Mr. Christopher had been smoking in the courtyard as he passed by. If that.

"Two shots," the man said.

"From where?" Wyatt asked.

"Over there." He pointed to where Wyatt had just been standing with Sandi. The crime scene team was still there, sifting through things on the street.

"Start at the beginning," Noel said, and Wyatt cut his eyes to the sandy-haired man. He had a full head of hair, worked out for an hour every morning, and a wife and three kids at home. Wyatt had been invited to his house for dinner, and he liked Noel's wife and kids.

"I was sitting here," the man said, and Wyatt almost rolled his eyes.

"Sitting where?" Noel asked.

Wyatt's phone rang, but he still heard Mr. Christopher say, "Right here on the fountain wall."

Noel made a note in his tablet, and Wyatt said, "Be right back," so he could answer Deirdre's call. "I'm so sorry," he said in lieu of hello.

"I turned on the news," she said. "It's fine. You look beyond busy."

"I'll be lucky to get out of here before darkness falls." Wyatt sighed. "Raincheck?"

"Sure," she said. "I have a wedding this weekend, but after that, my workload is fairly open."

"I have no idea what my schedule is like," he said. "I'll talk to Norma in the morning." He loved the woman who ran his office, and he'd never minded that she knew the intricate details of his personal life.

"You know my number," Deirdre said, and Wyatt liked that she wasn't upset. She was mature enough to know that things came up, and Wyatt wished he'd been ready for a relationship when she'd first moved here.

"Talk soon," he said as a commotion erupted near the back of the ambulance. "I have to go." He didn't bother hanging up as he broke into a run. Deirdre would end the call, and Wyatt would be lucky not to lose his phone in the sprint.

"Ma'am," he said while two of his officers held a woman back from trying to leap into the back of the ambulance and throttle the man who'd been driving the car.

She yelled something he couldn't discern, and Eli pushed her back again. "Ma'am, calm down," the officer commanded. "I *will* arrest you."

The woman fell back, and Wyatt recognized her as he arrived on the scene. "Bella," he barked. "Come with me."

The woman who had once been his late wife's friend turned toward him. Her face held a furious flush, and she panted. "Wyatt."

"Now." He gestured for her to come toward him, which she did. "The last thing you need is an arrest," he said as they moved away from the ambulance and the other officers. "Think about Joey."

Her son was only ten, and Bella's divorce had happened right on the heels of Christine's death. Wyatt didn't know all the details, but he knew Bella had spent a lot of time in court, fighting her ex over custody of their son. If she got arrested, that would seal her fate.

"I'm sorry," she said. "But that man tried to kill my sister."

Wyatt waved to another detective, indicating he should come over right now. "Wait a second. I want someone else to hear this too."

Tom came over, and Wyatt said, "This is Tom Pilfer. He's a detective with my department. Tom, Bella Murphy. She says the driver tried to kill her sister."

"Is that right?" Tom tapped on his tablet before he looked up. "Why do you think that?"

Wyatt stayed right next to him as he questioned Bella, who went on to tell a tale about an ex-boyfriend of her sister's who'd been showing up at work, sending her letters, and leaving things in her car for the past six months.

"And now he tried to drive his car into her office." She pointed to the car still halfway inside the building. "That's her office right there. She works at the desk next to the window. I know it was him."

Wyatt watched the photographer taking pictures from every angle of the entrance, the car, the building, the fountain, all of it. Pictures were crucial to an investigation, as sometimes cases went cold and when new investigators picked up the photos, they saw something the initial detectives hadn't noticed or didn't think was appropriate.

He'd solved a cold case in his early days as a detective

by examining an old crime scene photo with a bottle of mayonnaise sitting on a chair near the front door. It had only taken one question—*why was that there?*—to spark a lead that led to a fingerprint on the jar of mayo that had identified a murderer in a case that had been twelve years old.

"What's his name?"

"Stephen Villalobos," Bella said. "And he's in the ambulance."

The driver's name *was* Stephen Villalobos, and Wyatt's police instincts were firing like cannons.

"What's your sister's name?" Tom asked.

Bella gave it as "McKenna Lotus."

"Is she here?" Wyatt looked around. "Who's she talking to?"

"She's inside," Bella said. "I came as soon as she called me, and when she told me it was Stephen, I freaked out." She held up both hands. "I'm fine now. I'm fine." She wiped her bangs back off her forehead and blew out her breath. "I'm fine."

"Tom," Wyatt said. "Get Noel and go talk to Miss Lotus."

"You got it, boss." The detective walked away, and Wyatt stood there with Bella as he surveyed the scene. It was a huge space to canvas and cover, with people coming in and out every second.

He was very good at locking down a crime scene, and he'd trained his people to do the same. But there were

witnesses to contain, and forensic investigators, and officers, paramedics, and even firemen. And Bella had
gotten past his blocks, and she clearly hadn't been on-site
before the accident.

"Chief." Norma's voice came through his ear.

"Go ahead," he said.

"Press conference in forty-five minutes?"

His muscles tightened and then he sighed. "Yes," he
said. "Spread the word that it'll be on the steps in front
of the courthouse, same as it usually is." That would get
the media away from the crime scene, where they
currently circled like sharks just beyond the yellow
caution tape.

He'd do the press conference, and he'd make sure this
crime scene was picked clean and absolutely pristine
before anyone else left. Wyatt was getting a bit old to pull
an all-nighter, but he'd do it if he had to. *Anything for the
job*, that was what Christine had always said.

Hopefully, he'd get a moment to talk to Norma about
his schedule and get a dinner date with Deirdre on the
calendar before too much time passed.

"Chief," someone said, and Wyatt was getting really
tired of the word.

But he turned toward the man and said, "Yep," just
like he always did. After all, the Chief of Police didn't get
to do whatever he wanted, whenever he wanted. He was
a public face, and everyone on the island of Getaway Bay
would be watching to see how this situation was handled.

So he'd handle it with professionalism and power, the way he'd been doing for years now. Hopefully, Deirdre would wait for him and be available when he was able to call and make another date with her.

Chapter Six

Deirdre stayed up late to watch Wyatt on TV, and that was when she knew she had a serious crush on the man. "Of course you do," she muttered to herself as she got up with her empty coffee cup. She'd known that from the moment she'd met him.

He'd always made her heart pulse faster, and she liked that he was older than her by five years, had silver in his hair, and had held a steady job for years. She liked that she could see him on the television, and the way his uniform enunciated his tall, athletic figure, and the way his voice made her heart hum.

"Why did you turn him down on Friday?" Deirdre moaned as she put her coffee cup in the sink. Her routine included dishes in the morning, so she left the mug with the pot and pan she'd used to make dinner, and the plate she'd eaten it off of.

She'd boxed up the leftovers and planned to take

them to Wyatt's office in the morning. He was still at work at ten-thirty at night, and she hoped he'd appreciate the food. She knew she would have.

And maybe *she* could talk to Norma about the Chief's schedule.

The moment she thought it, she dismissed the thought. She wasn't going to set up a date with the man through his secretary.

She was just tired, as she didn't normally stay up late just to watch the news. She went to bed, hoping Wyatt would be able to very soon as well.

In the morning, Deirdre went through her routines of taking her vitamins, doing her dishes, and setting out food and water for the stray cats on the lane. She picked up the food for Wyatt and headed out. The police station seemed abnormally busy, as she couldn't even find a parking space in the lot.

"He's too busy," she said, and she didn't think anyone would like having non-essential personnel on the premises that morning. So she continued on to Your Tidal Forever with his food on her passenger seat. She could store it in the fridge in the kitchen until after work.

The moment she entered the building, Sunny stood up from her desk. "Deirdre," she said. "I just talked to Cindi from Jungle Plants. She said she can get your vines if you're still interested."

"No way." Deirdre beamed at Sunny and started laughing. "Thank you, Sunny."

"I just answered the phone." But she grinned like

she'd personally procured the vines Deirdre needed for the wedding.

"I'm so glad I didn't find anything at the craft store yesterday," she said. "And now I need to re-call my bride." Though Katelin and Hiro were pretty low-key, Deirdre still hadn't liked delivering the bad news only days before their big event.

"She called too, and she said she knew you wouldn't be in yet, but she wants to talk to you today."

"I'll call her now," Deirdre said, taking the two slips of paper from Sunny though the messages had already been delivered. She dialed Katelin on her way to her office, forgetting to take the food to the fridge so she set it on her desk as her bride answered.

"Katelin," Deirdre said brightly. "How are you this morning?"

"Good," she said. "Did you see the news about the car who drove into the building?"

"Yes," Deirdre said. Everyone on the island had likely heard about it, as the city had shut down two square blocks last night and still hadn't reopened them yet. She'd had to detour out of the way to get to work, but she hadn't really paid attention to why.

"Hiro's brother got injured, and he doesn't want to be in the wedding party in a cast."

"It's no problem," Deirdre said, realizing the wide reach of the accident. "We'll just position him in the back or something."

"He's got some cuts on his face," Katelin said.

"I'm so sorry," Deirdre said. "You're not postponing or anything?"

"Heavens, no," Katelin said. "The waiting list for the Waterford Waves Beach is thirteen months long."

Deirdre smiled and said, "It's going to be beautiful. And good news: The vines will be in on time, and we'll make sure you have the most spectacular wedding ever."

Katelin shrieked. "The vines will be in?"

"Yes, I just got a call about them," Deirdre couldn't help feeding off Katelin's excitement for greenery.

"That's great news!" She laughed. "Thanks, Deirdre."

"Do you have a replacement for Toa?"

"No, he's just going to sit or stand in the back. I feel bad for Hiro, but he says he doesn't care."

In Deirdre's experience, the groom didn't cause a lot of trouble. It was always the bride, and as long as Katelin was happy, Deirdre would be too. "Okay, well, let me know if anything else changes. I'll send a note to the photographer about Toa."

"Thanks, Deirdre." The call ended, and Deirdre got up to go put Wyatt's food in the fridge.

"Meeting in five," Meg said the moment Deirdre left her office.

"What meeting?"

"Hope texted this morning," Meg said, and Deirdre's shoulders shrank. She wasn't terribly busy right now, as she didn't have any holiday weddings or events coming up. Not like Meg, who had two high-profile weddings in front of her. Deirdre had this one this weekend, and then a two-hundred-person party for Software Solutions, the parent company for half a dozen apps, including Getaway Bay Singles.

Deirdre had downloaded the app but had never used it. Her relationship with Wyatt had begun, and while it would end only five weeks later, Deirdre knew by then that she didn't want to jump right into the dating pool.

In fact, though she'd been here for a year and a half now, she still wasn't sure she should be perpetuating something with anyone, let alone the Chief of Police.

What would he think of her permanent restraining order? That she couldn't be within three hundred feet of her own daughter? He'd want the whole story, and Deirdre hadn't told it to anyone.

Only a trusted few knew she had a daughter she didn't talk to, and they certainly didn't know it was because by law, she couldn't. No one knew that.

And you'll have to tell Wyatt.

She went to the kitchen and put the food in the fridge before pulling out her phone and checking it. Sure enough, Hope had texted an hour ago to call a staff meeting, and Deirdre couldn't believe she'd missed it.

Sometimes she didn't check her phone, because it only served as a reminder that her family didn't call or text. But Hope had a special chime, and Deirdre hadn't heard it that morning.

Maybe she'd been too distracted with thoughts of Wyatt.

Just as she was now.

She drew in a deep breath and turned toward the conference room. The sun shone in through the wall of windows, and Deirdre took a long breath as she reminded herself how wonderful it was to be alive.

"Morning," Hope said a moment later. "Let's all sit down, please. We have several new assignments to hand out." She was all-business in her navy blue skirt suit, and Deirdre always felt underdressed in comparison to her.

To most of the women who worked at Your Tidal Forever. But Hope had never commented on her choice of muted slacks and a brightly colored blouse. That was as dressed up as Deirdre got, and she didn't even wear jewelry or cute shoes.

She took a seat next in between Meg and Lisa, her best friends at Your Tidal Forever, and Lisa instantly put a slip of paper in front of her.

You and the CoP? Woooow.

A smiley face adorned the note, and Deirdre looked up at Lisa. She knew her husband was one of Wyatt's friends, and while Cal and Lisa had offered to set Deirdre and Wyatt up again, Deirdre certainly didn't need that.

She flipped over the piece of paper and scrawled a note back quickly. *How did you find out?*

Lisa read the words and rolled her eyes. Hope had started the meeting, but Lisa leaned toward Deirdre and whispered, "He's the Chief of Police, honey. Everyone knows."

"That's not possible," Deirdre whispered back. "We

haven't even gone out yet." She kept her eyes on Hope so she could straighten up the moment her boss looked at her.

"Fine." Lisa grinned and held out her palm.

"What?"

"I know you have lemon drops in your pocket."

Deirdre shook her head and smiled as she dug in her pocket for one of the individually wrapped delicacies she took everywhere with her. She placed it in Lisa's palm, who quickly unwrapped it and popped it into her mouth. With lemony fresh breath, she said. "Wyatt called Cal last night."

Surprise ran through Deirdre as Hope put the first new account up on the screen behind her. Another wedding. Deirdre liked weddings just fine, because they'd helped her grow and stretch in her party planning abilities. Before she'd come to Your Tidal Forever, she'd only done anniversary parties and birthday parties. Something with a family, maybe up to twenty or thirty people.

The firm she'd worked for in Seattle didn't do receptions or weddings, and she'd enjoyed learning a new skill set. But weddings and receptions came with a lot more stress than a company party or a couple's fiftieth anniversary party.

For some reason, she didn't want to pick up another wedding, but she reached for a bid sheet from the middle of the table, same as everyone else.

These roundtable meetings worked the same every time Hope called them. She presented the available gigs, all of which came with a different payday. The planners in the room would mark the ones they were capable of doing after looking at their schedules and other things, and all the papers would get turned in. Hope would take five minutes—literally, not a second more—to shuffle through them, and then everyone left with their assignments.

Deirdre's upcoming schedule was very light, as she'd missed the last meeting and therefore hadn't gotten any new assignments. So she already knew without consulting her calendar that she could do the DeGraw wedding. She checked the box in front of the name and sat back while Lisa continued to whisper about the brief phone call between the two men.

Deirdre honestly didn't know how Wyatt had time to make personal calls, especially during stressful situations. Surely he hadn't gotten home until very late. But he was a man of many talents and many mysteries, and she hoped she'd get a call from him soon.

Another wedding. Two reception-onlys. A yacht party. Deirdre checked them all.

"And lastly, Norma Mumford from the police station called this morning. She wants to put together a holiday party for the Chief and everyone in the department, and she wants one of us to do it."

Police department flashed up on the wall, and Deirdre's heartbeat started to ricochet through her whole body.

"Oh," Lisa said, and she leaned toward Shannon, who sat on the other side of her. Deirdre's whole world narrowed to those two words, and she had the keen urge to erase all of the other checkmarks on her paper and leave only the one for this particular party.

That way, if Wyatt was astronomically busy with what was now being labeled as a shooting, she could still have a reason to see him.

Why, oh why had she said no to dinner on Friday night with him?

She gave herself a mental shake as Hope said, "One more minute to check things, ladies. I have a client coming in ten minutes." She was nothing if not efficient, and Deirdre panicked as she looked down at her paper.

She could take on one of the weddings, a reception, and this party. But she didn't want the police department party to get overshadowed by something else.

Her fingers trembled as she tried to figure out what to do. What to erase. She hurried to remove the check mark in front of the yacht party and one of the weddings. She now had checks in front of one wedding, both receptions, and the department party.

"Papers," Hope called, and Lisa reached over and plucked Deirdre's away before she could do anything else.

She gasped in protest but didn't say anything else. And her paper was gone now anyway. Lisa took her pen too and put it in the glass jar in the center of the table. "What's wrong?" she asked as she settled back into her seat. "You're going to get a couple of these."

"It's not...."

"My schedule is jammed," Lisa said. "I didn't mark any."

"Can you do that?"

"Of course," Lisa said. "I already have four weddings from now until Valentine's Day. I can't take on anything else, even a yacht party." She crossed her legs and said something to Shannon.

Deirdre watched Hope put the papers in separate piles, and she didn't take the full five minutes this time. "All right, ladies," she said. "Let's start at the beginning. The DeGraw wedding goes to Deirdre."

Her heart fell to her non-cute shoes, but she smiled and nodded. Shannon passed her a file while Hope said, "The Joplin wedding is going to Charlotte. The Peterson reception is Deirdre's."

Another fake smile. Another file folder of information she'd have to absorb and go over. More meetings with brides, grooms, and mothers.

"The Watkins reception is Tina's. The yacht party for Mike Billings is Shannon's. And the police department party is going to Deirdre." She looked up. "Deirdre, that's three new things for you. You'd checked a lot. You sure this is okay?"

"Yes," she managed to croak out.

"I could give the department party to Lisa...." Hope studied the papers again. "But you're the only one who signed up for it." She raised her eyes to Deirdre's again, clear questions in hers.

Lisa giggled, and Deirdre knew that she'd done something. Probably passed the word around the table for everyone to leave that one for her. She'd gotten messages like that before for some of the girls and she'd left her name off jobs she could've taken.

"It's fine," she said. "The weddings aren't for months, and I can focus on the department party now."

"Yeah, you can," Lisa whispered, and Deirdre's face grew hot.

"All right," Hope said as her phone chimed out an alarm. "We're done. Shannon has all the preliminary notes from Sunny. Let's make today awesome, ladies." The meeting broke up, but Deirdre stayed in her seat as Shannon passed her the last folder.

"Norma wants you to call as soon as you can," Shannon said. "But honestly, they're swamped over there right now. Maybe give it a day or two, but definitely call by the end of the week."

"Okay." Deirdre flipped open the folder and looked at the intake sheet.

Lisa leaned toward her and said, "Go get 'im, Deirdre. He's great."

She nodded, because she already knew Wyatt was great. Part of her was thrilled she'd gotten the job. She needed the work, and three new events would keep her plenty busy for a while. The other part of her didn't want to have a business relationship with Wyatt at all, and that was the part with the loudest wail.

Would he ever ask her out now? Or would they just spend evenings in his office, some variety of delivered food on the desk between them while they talked about what kind of finger foods he wanted for the holiday party?

And when she saw Norma Mumford as the contact person for the party, her enthusiasm for the project blew away like brittle leaves in a stiff wind.

Of course Wyatt wouldn't be the one to sit down with the party planner. He didn't even keep his own schedule. Norma really ran the police department, and Deirdre would be lucky if she even saw Wyatt when she went to meet with the woman.

She finally got up when she realized she was the only person left in the conference room. Back in her office, she closed the door and layered the folders on top of each other in the order in which she'd received them. She'd go through them one by one, the way she always did. Nothing was special about the police department file. Nothing special at all.

Chapter Seven

Wyatt had slept for two hours of the last thirty-six. So when Norma entered his office in the late afternoon with a cup of coffee and his favorite cream cheese Danish from a hole-in-the-wall bakery, he almost growled at her.

"You never come bearing afternoon snacks unless you want something," he said, taking the coffee but refusing to take a sip. The scent of it had his mouth watering though, and he had a killer headache he knew the caffeine would tame.

"Now, Wyatt," she said sitting down and leaning back in her chair. "We've talked about this one before."

"Is it related to the possible shooting?"

"Nope."

He took a sip of the coffee, the hot liquid calming him instantly. "All right. Shoot."

"It's the department holiday party."

Wyatt glared at her deliberately and picked up the pastry. "Go on."

"You won't have to do anything," she said with a smile. "I hired a party planner this year."

"Do we have a budget for that?"

"Yes," Norma said simply. "And she'll take care of everything for the party. And I'll take care of her." She removed a piece of paper from her skirt pocket and smoothed it against her leg while Wyatt took a bite of his snack.

He moaned as the flaky pastry and sweet cream cheese filled his mouth. Norma simply smiled at him, and Wyatt realized he wasn't out of the woods yet. And he'd accepted her gifts already.

"I just need you to sign this," she said. "And then you should go home. There's nothing else to do today anyway. Feed Tigger and go to bed."

Going to bed sounded fantastic, and Wyatt would do what his secretary said. Norma had never led him astray, and she put the paper on his desk. He didn't reach for it but continued to eat.

"Did you want to see your schedule too?" she asked. "I just remembered." She jumped to her feet and started for the door before he could protest. Yes, he'd asked her for his schedule so he could set something up with Deirdre. But he'd had more time to think about it, and perhaps their relationship just wasn't in the cards. Perhaps fate had other plans for Wyatt. He wished his heart would get memos from fate, though, as it would save him some embarrassment and frustration.

He pulled the budget approval form toward him and read the top. One thousand dollars to Your Tidal Forever. His heart started pounding. Deirdre worked for Your Tidal Forever, and Wyatt thought they just did weddings.

Norma re-entered the office, her huge planner in her hands. "All right," she said.

"Your Tidal Forever?" he asked.

She glanced up, surprise in her hazel eyes. "What?"

He held up the budget request form. "I thought Your Tidal Forever planned weddings." He *knew* they did. He'd hired them to plan Jennifer's wedding, and they'd done an amazing job.

"Oh." Norma's voice sounded false as she sat down and balanced her date book on her knees. "They do. But they do other things too. Anniversary parties. Receptions. And company parties."

Wyatt looked down at the paper again. "Who's doing the department party?"

"Um, let's see," Norma said. "You have Friday night open for a dinner appointment."

Wyatt glanced up, only catching sight of the top of Norma's head because she was studying her book. "Norma," he said, and he waited until she looked at him. "Who's doing the department party from Your Tidal Forever?"

"It doesn't matter," Norma said, swallowing. Wyatt knew then that something was definitely afoot. "You're not going to be working with them. I am." She held up her book. "Friday night? Dinner with Deirdre?"

"I thought I had that dinner with the commissioner on Friday."

"That's next Friday. This Friday is open."

"Fine," he said. "I'll call her." He reached for his phone, intending to ask her about a lot more than dinner on Friday. After all, there could only be one reason Norma didn't want to tell him who she was working with for the party.

The call went to voicemail, and he said, "Hey, Deirdre, it's Wyatt." He paused as if she were on the line, because Norma wouldn't know. "Quick question: Do you know who's doing the department party for us?"

Norma lunged forward and reached for his phone. He let her take it, a chuckle starting down inside his chest.

"Deirdre, I didn't tell him, I swe—" She pulled the phone away from her ear. "She's not there." She tapped to end the call, practically slamming his phone on the desk in the next moment. "You little sneak."

He leaned back in his chair and folded his arms. "So Deirdre is planning the department party."

"Yes."

"Why couldn't you just tell me?" Wyatt's adrenaline, combined with the coffee, really had his cells buzzing. Deirdre was planning the department party. That meant he'd get to see her more often, while he worked.

"She asked me not to."

"Why would she do that?"

"She didn't want your relationship—" His phone rang, and she reached for it instead of finishing her explanation. "It's her."

Wyatt gestured for her to take the call. "By all means. Explain everything to her. She's probably confused about that message."

"Deirdre," Norma said, her professional tone hitched in place. "It's Norma, dear. Yes, he's right here…yes, he knows." Her eyes widened, and she shook her head. "Yes, all right." She held the phone out to him. "She'd like to speak to you."

"It *is* my phone." He reached for it and gave Norma a knowing look as he put the phone to his ear. "Hey, sweetheart."

"Sweetheart?" Deirdre asked. "Okay, never mind. Look, I just need to know if you're okay with me working with Norma on the department party or not."

"Why wouldn't I be okay with that?"

"I…don't know."

"Would you like to go to dinner on Friday?" he asked.

Deirdre remained silent for several long moments. "Wyatt, I'm confused."

"Why didn't you want to tell me you were planning the party? Norma said you asked her not to tell me."

"Because." She sighed. "I didn't want our relationship to be professional."

A smile filled his whole face, and Norma grinned too. "So dinner on Friday would work for you." He lifted his eyebrows, and Norma glanced down at the date book, nodding.

"Yes," Deirdre said.

"I can't guarantee that there won't be a shooting or something," he said. "But I'm really hoping to make it this time."

"Me too, Wyatt. I have food for you, and I'm leaving the office now to meet with a client at a reception center. Is now a good time to drop by?"

Wyatt scanned his desk, which held an assortment of candy wrappers and old coffee mugs. "Yes," he said. "Now is a great time to drop by." He stood up and picked up one of the old cups, dropping it in the trash can. Norma did the same, sweeping the wrappers into her hand all at once.

"Great," Deirdre said. "I'll see you in a few."

Wyatt put his phone down so he could use both hands to clean up his desk. "Does it smell bad in here?"

"Yes," Norma said. "I'll grab the air freshener."

He looked up at her. "Can you leave me a couple week's worth of appointments, so I can see what else I have coming up?"

Norma grinned at him the way a wolf would grin at its next meal. "You really like this woman, don't you?"

Wyatt stacked his folders. "Was that not obvious from the way I've just cleaned up my desk?"

Norma burst out laughing, and she moved toward the door. "I'll call a maid service for your house too, as you have Saturday free as well, and who knows? Maybe you'd like to introduce Deirdre to Tigger." With that, she left the office, and Wyatt looked down, trying to remember what he'd been working on when she'd come into his office fifteen minutes ago.

His brain felt like mush, and he decided he'd get the food from Deirdre, solidify their plans for Friday night, and head home to sleep.

While he waited, he went through his email, one of his most dreaded chores. He'd answered a few and deleted countless others before Deirdre walked in, the words, "Good afternoon, Wyatt," dripping from that pretty mouth.

"Deirdre," he said, practically overturning his desk in his haste to stand up. His knee cracked on the bottom of the desk, and he almost swore. He managed to keep calm as he rounded his desk and took the paper bag of food from her.

She wore an expensive pair of black slacks with a yellow and orange striped blouse, along with a hint of teasing in those electric blue eyes. Her blonde hair fell over her shoulders in easy waves, and Wyatt wanted to run his fingers through it.

He hadn't kissed her last time they'd dated, as he'd been terrified of cheating on his wife. Everything about last time he and Deirdre tried a relationship embarrassed him, and he hoped she had a bad memory.

But he knew she didn't. The woman was sharp and smart and sexy, and Wyatt had liked her from the moment he'd met her, months and months ago.

"Thank you," he finally remembered to say. "I'm sure this will be delicious. I remember you being a good cook."

"I don't remember you ever eating anything I've made," she said, smiling at him. Maybe he'd just caught her at a bad time on Friday, because she seemed open and receptive to him now.

"Maybe I haven't," he said. "But it'll be better than anything I could've ordered tonight."

"Oh, come on," she said with a laugh. "That's not true. Even the chicken sandwiches from Poultry Palace are better than what you're holding."

Wyatt's stomach growled at the thought of a crispy chicken sandwich and fries for dinner. "Do you have time for dinner tonight?"

"I'm meeting a client," she said, stepping closer to him. She reached out and put her hand on his bicep. "But I'm available Friday, if it's a bit later. I have a wedding all day Saturday, and I usually have some last-minute emergency to take care of that keeps me late on Friday." She watched him with those eyes, and while they were bright and electric, Wyatt would also classify them as soulful.

"Later is fine," he said through a narrow throat.

"Let's plan on eight," she said. "I can't remember the last time I worked that late."

"Sounds good," he said. "I'll pick you up, and you'll tell me where you want to go."

"Deal," she said, stepping even closer. So close, Wyatt

had to drop his chin to keep eye contact. "I hope it works out this time, Wyatt."

"Me too," he murmured. He would make sure it worked out. How, he didn't know, but he'd do everything in his power to be available at eight p.m. on Friday night.

Deirdre lifted onto her toes and swept her lips across his cheek. "See you then." She turned and left his office while Wyatt stared after her. Numb, he lifted his fingers to where her mouth had burned him, in complete wonder at this woman.

No, he was in complete awe about his *feelings* for this woman. He'd been so in love with Christine, and they'd been married for twenty years before he'd lost her. He'd never looked at another woman and never been tempted away from his wife.

For years after her death, he hadn't even known how he felt—happy, sad, mad, frustrated, satisfied. Nothing. He'd simply disappeared emotionally. Sometimes mentally, too. Sometimes he'd find himself staring at a file, and he had no idea how long he'd been doing it. He couldn't remember the last time he'd showered. That kind of thing.

Slowly, with the help of his officers, his friends, his daughter, and his grief meetings, Wyatt had pulled himself back into some semblance of a human being.

He dropped his hand, grabbed his laptop from his desk, and followed Deirdre out the door. "Norma," he said, stopping by her desk. "Please don't call me unless it's a major emergency."

"You got it, Chief."

"Remind me what the major emergencies are."

"Major crime—shooting, bombing, smuggling. Officer down. Or your mother calling." She beamed up at him, and Wyatt nodded.

"Have a good night, Norma."

"You too, Chief."

Wyatt planned to simply eat and collapse into bed, his thoughts revolving around the beautiful Deirdre Bernard.

Chapter Eight

Deirdre set up a time to meet with Norma about the police department party on her way out of Wyatt's office on Tuesday afternoon. She had all of her hands on-deck for the Clawson wedding that weekend, and she wouldn't be returning to the station until the following week.

Luckily, Wyatt seemed interested in her and willing to give her another chance after her rejection last weekend. Their date for Friday night crept closer and closer, until finally the day dawned bright and beachy, just like it usually did in Getaway Bay.

Deirdre arrived at Your Tidal Forever early, before even Sunny, who seemed perpetually perched at the desk in the lobby. She got a great hour of work finished before anyone else stepped foot in the building, and she turned her attention to her next clients.

She already had the initial meeting set up with

Norma, but she should make contact with her next bride. She leafed through the folder to find the name of the woman she'd be working with for the next six months to make sure she got the wedding of her dreams.

After finding the number, she made the call to Michelle DeGraw, who answered the phone on the second ring. "You're from Your Tidal Forever, aren't you?" she asked, her words running together. "Oh my goodness, I'm so excited. *So* excited. You have no idea. I've been saving for three years for this wedding, so I could hire you." She took a deep breath, and Deirdre probably should've interjected. But she didn't know what to say.

"I know the wedding isn't until next April, but I'm ready to get started now. My fiancé is off-island right now, but you don't need to meet him to get started, do you? I mean, Johnny said he doesn't even care what I do for the wedding. So...."

"Michelle," Deirdre said, shaking her head and laughing a little. "I'm glad you're excited for your wedding. I'm thrilled to be working with you. I'm Deirdre Bernard, and I'm going to be your wedding planner." She tapped on her laptop to get the screen to brighten back up. "You're going to get your tidal forever, I can promise you that. Why don't you tell me a little bit about yourself, and we'll see if we can get something on the schedule for next week."

"Okay," Michelle said. "I'm Michelle DeGraw, and I work as a pediatric dental assistant in East Bay. I love working with kids, and I love dogs." Breath. "And Johnny and I met at a dog training camp. He had this huge schnauzer. You should've seen it!" Breath. "Anyway...."

Deirdre wondered if she'd gotten in over her head as Michelle continued to talk. A few minutes later, she said, "I can take a half-day off on Wednesday if that works for you?"

She looked at her calendar, which was fairly wide open, and said, "One o'clock? I can order in lunch."

Michelle squealed, and Deirdre pressed her eyes closed until she stopped. "I can't wait!"

"Me either," Deirdre said. She sighed as she set her phone on her desk. Most brides were enthusiastic about their own weddings, and Michelle wasn't that different from most of the other women Deirdre had served.

An alarm went off on her phone, and she silenced it. She pressed her palms against the desk and drew in a deep breath. "Game time." She left her office and stuck her head into Meg's. "You ready?"

She held up one finger, and Deirdre saw she was on the phone. She held up both palms in surrender and continued down the hall to Hope's office. But it was dark, and Shannon wasn't at her desk either.

Deirdre turned around as the sound of heels clicking toward her, and Shannon smiled. "I have the key," she said, holding it out in front of her. "You better get going. I heard the setup for this is elaborate."

"I've done it twice this week," Deirdre said. "It's going to go great." She took the key from Shannon with a smile. "And be honest. Did you give me Michelle DeGraw as punishment for missing the last meeting?" She tried to hold back her giggle, but it came spilling out.

Shannon laughed too. "She's exuberant, isn't she?"

"Excitable," Deirdre said.

"Enthusiastic." Shannon took her place behind her desk.

Deirdre laughed again. "You win." She indicated Hope's dark office. "Hope's not in?"

"She and Aiden had an appointment." Shannon met Deirdre's eye, and they both nodded.

"Good for them," Deirdre said. "I hope it works for them." She pocketed the key and retraced her steps back to Meg's office.

She tossed her laptop in her huge purse and looked up. "I'm ready."

"Where are we going for lunch?" Deirdre asked as her friend walked toward her.

"The Liaison," Meg said.

"Really?" Deirdre asked. "They don't even have anything worth eating there." The Liaison served "healthy food you can feel good about eating," but it didn't actually *taste* good. And Deirdre was too old to put something in her mouth that didn't bring her great satisfaction.

"You said you'd buy me lunch at the establishment of my choice if I helped you set up." Meg gave her a pointed look as she passed Deirdre and left her office. "I mean, without me, will you even make it to your dinner

72

date with the ultra-hot Chief of Police tonight?" She really hit the T on the last word, and Deirdre rolled her eyes.

"Ultra-hot?" She followed Meg down the hall to the back exit, where the vans were kept. They had half a dozen stops to make to pick up the supplies, from the chair sleeves to the flowers to the fish bowls which Deirdre would lovingly fill with water and then delicately drop floating candles onto the surface. The addition of real fire always warmed a space, and Deirdre couldn't wait to see everything come together for the nuptials tomorrow.

This afternoon though, all she needed to do was make sure the party rental company showed up with the right tents and the correct number of chairs. She and Meg would dress everything up, and then tomorrow morning, they'd finish with lighting the candles and arranging all of the flowers just-so.

"Please," Meg said. "If you can't admit that your new boyfriend is ultra-hot, you need to get your eyes checked."

"One, he's not my boyfriend," Deirdre said. She wasn't seventeen years old. "Two, I prefer the word *handsome*. He's ultra-*handsome*." He wasn't seventeen either.

"Fine," Meg said. "I can get on-board with that description." They climbed into the van, and Deirdre put her purse between the two bucket seats up front. "Are you so excited for tonight?"

"You know what?" Deirdre asked. "I am. Now, help

me decide where to go—and do *not* say The Liaison. I want to get a second date."

————

DEIRDRE TUGGED ON A PAIR OF CUTE ANKLE BOOTS, anxious as Wyatt was set to arrive any moment. Sure enough, the doorbell rang before she'd zipped up the second boot, and she hurried to finish the job. Jumping to her feet, she darted out of her bedroom and down the hall, calling, "Coming."

She pulled open the door, her heart racing in her chest. Wyatt stood there, tall and broad and utterly charming with that small smile on his face and all that salt peppered in his dark hair.

"Evening, Deirdre," he said, his deep voice strumming something deep inside her stomach.

"Hey," she said. "I'm almost ready. You wanna come in?"

"Sure." He stepped into her house as she inched back, still holding the door. She closed it behind him and went to get her purse.

"I just need my bag and to make sure I have lights on, so I don't have to come home in the dark."

"Smart."

Deirdre's cells rioted as she reached for a switch to flood the kitchen with light. She smiled at Wyatt as she turned, and her ankle buckled in the wedged boots. She grunted as she righted herself, her hand flying out to catch herself against the kitchen counter.

"You okay?" Wyatt asked, his hand landing on her arm too, as if he could steady her. Her skin sizzled where his met it, and she first looked at his fingers and then his face.

She swallowed, because she knew why she was so nervous. Yes, he was ultra-handsome and Deirdre was a tiny bit anxious because of that. She liked him a lot, and his opinion of her was very important to her.

And as soon as she told him about her daughter and the restraining order, she didn't think he'd fight quite so hard to be in her life.

"Deirdre?"

"I'm okay," she said quickly, sliding her hand away. He removed his fingers from her arm and backed up a step.

"Where are we going for dinner?"

"The Indian House?" Why she'd phrased it as a question, she wasn't sure. "Do you like Indian food?"

"Love it," he said. "Are you ready?"

"Yes." She preceded him to the door, and relief spread through her when she saw he'd driven his own car. A civilian Jeep. Not his police cruiser. The last thing she needed was every eye in Getaway Bay on her for a simple dinner date.

They'd texted quite a bit over the last three days, but Chief Wyatt had a strict ten p.m. bedtime that he did not break. Deirdre had trouble sleeping after their late-night texting sessions, and she wondered if it might have been easier to tell him about Emma and the restraining order via text instead of face-to-face.

But she'd been worried that this face-to-face dinner would be called off if she did, and while she'd said no to his dinner invitation a week ago, she now found herself desperately wanting to see if they could make a relationship work this time.

He helped her into the Jeep, which was quite the step up in her wedges, his hand warm on her lower back. "Tell him," she muttered to herself as he rounded the hood and opened the driver's side door.

"Wyatt," she said.

He started the vehicle and looked at her.

"I have to tell you something." She slicked her palms down the front of her jeans. Deirdre hated feeling like this. The nerves. The uncertainty. The guilt. The shame.

She'd sat in a courtroom and felt this level of unease. She really disliked being falsely accused, and she couldn't stand that sometimes there was injustice in the justice system.

"Deirdre," he said. "If you don't want to go out with me, it's fine."

"I do," she said, finally forcing herself to look fully at him. His dark eyes drank her up, and Deirdre could get lost for a good long while in eyes like that. "It's not that."

"What is it then?"

"You're a public figure, right?"

"Oh, boy," he said.

"People like to dig into the past of people like you."

"It's not an elected position," he said. "I'm not the Sheriff."

"But you can't date like, a criminal or anything."

Wyatt opened his mouth to speak but promptly shut it again. His eyes held a new glint now, and Deirdre could see the detective in him. "Deirdre?"

"I have a restraining order against me," she said. "My daughter filed it, and though it's pretty much a load of crap, it still got approved because I called her cell phone before the hearing. I thought I had the phone in my car, and I couldn't find it. I wanted to give it back to her father, but that violated the temporary order, and the judge didn't care that I thought I had the phone. He said it was an attempt to contact her, when I'd been ordered not to." She was aware that she'd turned into Michelle DeGraw, talking faster and faster without breathing.

She took a long breath and slowed down. "That's why I don't talk to my daughter. When all of that happened, I moved to Getaway Bay."

He said nothing, those police eyes searching her face.

"So I understand if *you* don't want to go out with *me*," she said, her heart wailing a little bit at the prospect of losing him before she'd really had a chance to be with him. He hadn't been ready last time, and she'd blown him off last weekend.

Finally, Wyatt flipped the Jeep into reverse and backed out of her driveway. "Indian House? My wife loves the butter chicken there. What's your favorite dish?"

Chapter Nine

Wyatt hadn't been sure what would happen at dinner that night, but he certainly hadn't expected to hear the beautiful blonde say she had a protective order against her.

At the same time, he knew sometimes those things were issued for suspect reasons.

"Loves?" Deirdre asked, and Wyatt felt whiplashed all around. He didn't drive the Jeep much, and he pushed on the brake too hard, sending them both toward the dash.

A nervous chuckle came out of his mouth. "Uh, I talk about Christine in the present tense," he said. "It was something I learned at grief counseling."

"Oh." She folded her arms and looked away, and Wyatt eased through the four-way stop. "You don't care about the protective order?"

"It's a civil matter," he said. "You're not a criminal."

He did want to hear more about why her minor daughter would file a protective order against her, but he wasn't going to ask. Deirdre would tell him when she was comfortable doing so.

"I would be, if I violated the order."

"But you haven't violated the order," he said. "I never would've known had you not told me."

"You wouldn't have run a background check on me?"

Wyatt laughed, some of the nerves dissipating now that he'd spent longer than five minutes with her. "Deirdre, I trust you."

"I heard some cops do that. You never can be too careful."

"Would you like me to run a background check on you?" He glanced at her, and a small smile played with that mouth as she shook her head no. Oh, that mouth. He wanted to kiss her so badly, and that sent his pulse running like a scared rabbit.

He hadn't kissed anyone but his wife in a very, very long time.

But the twinge of guilt that had been behind his heart last time he and Deirdre had tried a relationship wasn't there this time. Not even a tiny pinch.

So he was ready.

The real question was whether or not Deirdre could trust him enough to tell him all the intimate details of her life. She'd spoken true when she'd said he was a public figure. He felt like most people in Getaway Bay knew all about him already.

Maybe they didn't know his favorite color or how he preferred his eggs, but they knew enough.

"I miss Christine," he said. "She took care of everything for me, and she worked at the library a few days a week."

"I bet it is hard," she said. "Even though I was the one who filed for divorce, I missed my husband for the first few months."

"Did you?" Wyatt pulled into the parking lot at The Indian House. "I wonder why."

"I don't like being in the house alone at night," she said. "It was something I had to get used to." She looked at him, pure vulnerability on her face. "That was when I developed my obsession with lemon drops. I'd hear something in the house that scared me, and I'd pop in a lemon drop. I couldn't go look for an intruder until I finished it. And by then, I was usually asleep or absorbed back into my book."

"And clearly, still alive," Wyatt said, smiling.

"Clearly." Deirdre turned to her door and got out of his Jeep. They met at the front of the truck, and Wyatt slipped his hand into hers.

"So you love lemon drops. What do you dislike?" he asked.

"Tomatoes," she said. "You?"

"Scallops."

"Fascinating," she said. "Most people on the island love seafood."

"I love crab and lobster," he said. "Mahi mahi, especially with pineapple-mango relish. Shrimp. But there's something funky about the texture of a scallop."

"It's like seared, soft butter."

"Yeah," he said. "I feel like it's not done."

Deirdre giggled as he held the door open for her, and the scent of Indian spices met his nose. "Fair enough. What do you like here?"

"The butter chicken," he said. "And plenty of naan."

"Oh, the bread. Of course." She stepped up to the hostess station and gave the woman standing there her name. At least four couples waited on the couches, and Wyatt felt all of them look at him.

The woman—Nita Reddy—looked at him, and her eyes rounded. "Chief," she said. "Right this way."

"But—"

Wyatt squeezed Deirdre's hand to silence her, and he followed Nita past the podium. "Nita," he said. "There are other people."

"We have all the tables coming in minutes," she said over her shoulder.

"We can wait," Wyatt said, increasing his pace to step past Deirdre. "Really. Take the next person on the list."

Nita put the menus on a table and turned to Wyatt. "Is this okay?"

"No," he said. "You know I like a booth, and that I don't mind waiting my turn." Wyatt really should've called ahead to give Nita this talking-to. He didn't want to embarrass her, but he was embarrassed in front of Deirdre.

"Look, Krisha is already taking back two more couples," she said. "I'll go get the other two now." She swept her arm around the restaurant. "We have plenty of tables now. Our rush just ended."

"Wyatt," Deirdre said, picking up the menus. He watched as she smiled up at him. "If you have a booth, Nita," she said. "We'll sit down and get out of your hair."

"Right here." The Indian woman moved several feet to an empty booth and indicated it.

Wyatt let Deirdre lead him to it, and he sat with his back to the majority of the restaurant. Christine had teased him once that he was part feline, because he believed if he couldn't see people, they couldn't see him.

"Thank you," he said as Nita patted his shoulder. He took his time settling in and spreading the napkin across his lap. When he finally looked at Deirdre, she was watching him. "Sorry. I should've warned you about that."

"What's the story there?"

"Where?"

"With you and Nita Reddy."

"Oh, when Christine and I were first married, we lived on the same street as the Reddy's. Their daughters are quite a bit older than Jenn, and they'd come babysit or take her for walks or whatever. They opened The Indian House, and we were some of their first customers." He smiled at the fond memories, the old times. "So we go way back."

Deirdre kept all of her emotions behind a careful

mask, and Wyatt didn't like it. But he couldn't very well reach across the table and swipe it away. "That's great."

"She always tries to seat me before everyone," he said. "No matter how many times I tell her I don't mind waiting."

She looked out across the restaurant. "Well, they all have a table now, too, so I wouldn't worry about it too much."

That was because Deirdre didn't have to shoulder all the glances, all the eyes. Wyatt did, and had for years. But he wasn't going to argue with her.

"I suppose you want to know more about my daughter."

Wyatt picked up the menu, though he had the thing memorized. "Only if you want to tell me." He focused on the specialty drinks to give Deirdre a moment to organize her thoughts. A waitress arrived before she spoke, and Wyatt beamed up at the girl.

"Evening, Chief," she said, cutting a glance at Deirdre. "Your usual?"

"Yes, please," he said. "And I want the strawberry infused peach lemonade tonight. With two shots of cream." He handed Myra the menu and they both looked at Deirdre.

"I can see this is on," she said. "I want whatever his special is." She hadn't even picked up a menu. "And lots of Diet Coke."

Myra smiled at her and leaned closer to Wyatt. "She's pretty."

Wyatt could barely hear her, so Deirdre certainly couldn't. Still, a flush crawled up his neck as Myra walked away and Deirdre said, "What did she say?"

"She said you were pretty." Wyatt cleared his throat. "And she's right. You look great tonight." He couldn't remember if he'd told her or not.

"Just tonight?" she teased, and Wyatt relaxed a little bit. The heat in the restaurant shot up—or maybe that was all inside his body.

"Always," he said, smiling at her. "I'm glad we're finally doing this."

"No major incidents tonight," she said.

"Nope," he said. "And I'm not on-call."

"Who is?"

"My second," he said. "Jeff Alveada."

"I don't know him."

"Good guy," Wyatt said, wondering how to salvage this conversation. "So you're doing the department party." He wanted to kick himself in the teeth the moment the words left his mouth.

Deirdre's eyes shuttered for a moment, but then she blinked and looked at him. "Yep," she said. "But I don't want to talk about work."

"No?" Maybe if she led the conversation, he could get out of these dangerous waters.

"No." She leaned forward. "I'll talk fast, so we can then enjoy the food."

"You don't have to do that."

"I want to." She swallowed and sucked in a breath.

85

"After the divorce, I got full custody of Emma. She was only ten. By thirteen, she'd started drinking and hiding the vodka bottles in the top of her closet. I found them one day, and in her words, I 'freaked out'." She made air quotes around the last two words.

"I guess I threw the empty bottles and the glass shattered and we both stepped on some of it. She was crying, and she was so angry." Deirdre paused, her words no longer rushing over themselves. Her eyes took on a faraway quality that spoke of old memories too, but not the good kind.

She gave herself a little shake. "Anyway, she accused me of being overbearing and controlling, and she ran out." She pushed her breath out now, a great big sigh of air. "She walked the few miles to her father's, who called me, irate that Emma—a thirteen-year-old who had been drinking and partying in my house—had cuts on her feet. There were all these bloody pictures." She waved her hand, and Wyatt had no idea how a person dealt with all of this. From their only child.

"She wouldn't leave his house, but I had custody." Deirdre's eyes crackled with lightning, and Wyatt knew this was still a very hot topic for her. "So she got her dad to file a protective order against me, take her to the hospital, all of it."

"And she didn't have her phone."

"No, she left the house without it. Dalton was plenty mad about that too. He pays for a tracking feature on it, but she didn't have it. She could've been kidnapped, etcetera, etcetera." Deirdre wasn't making light of it, he could tell. She looked downright miserable. "All of that amounted to me being too controlling—her phone had been charging in the car—because I made her give up her devices by nine o'clock. That was what she told the judge. That she didn't have her phone because I was the Phone Nazi." More air quotes. Lots of bitterness. So many hurt feelings.

Wyatt reached across the table and took both of her hands in his. "I'm so sorry, Deirdre. I can see that this is very hard for you."

She practically sagged under the weight of the world. "It is."

"So you left the North Shore."

"It's a big place," she said. "As far as geography goes. Lots of beachfront and all that. But the actual physical places to shop and dine—not so many. If I ran into Emma at all, she could call the cops, and I could be arrested."

"You didn't fight the order?"

"I did," she said. "But Emma lied. She'd had Dalton take her to the hospital again, and she claimed I wouldn't take her to the doctor. I wouldn't let her go out with her friends. Basically, she accused me of beating her, hurting her, flying into violent rages, and being a prison warden."

She drew in a deep breath, and Wyatt wished he could take her pain from her. He'd been in the depths of sorrow too, but never accompanied by this much anger. Pain, sure. Grief. Misery. Depression. Anxiety. A sense of drowning, being so overwhelmed he'd never get caught up.

Yes to all of those.

He'd had a brief moment of anger, but it had only lasted a few weeks. If that.

Deirdre had been in Getaway Bay for about a year and a half. Still, his heart went out to her, and he looked down at the table, unsure of what else to say.

"Sorry," she said, her voice a little higher than normal. She pulled her hands out from under his and swiped at her face. "I'm fine. But there's the story."

"Thank you for telling me," he said.

Myra returned with their drinks, and the words, "Your food is right behind me," and that broke the tension at the table.

Wyatt leaned away as his platter of naan and butter chicken with a full serving of white rice and one of pork fried rice was set in front of him. A smile crossed his face, and he looked up to watch Deirdre's reaction to his "special."

"Oh, wow," she said, a smile painting over her pain. "This is a week's worth of food, Wyatt."

"Hey," he said, picking up his fork. "We all have secrets, don't we?"

Chapter Ten

Deirdre smiled to herself as she lit a pretty, pale pink candle and gently lowered it into the water. "There." That was the last one, and as she looked down the table, a sense of peace and joy filled her.

The vines were gorgeous, and false ones wouldn't have been nearly as stunning. Relief and gladness spread through her that Jungle Plants had been able to get the order in on time. Katelin was going to be radiant and beautiful too, and she deserved a dance, dinner, and reception to match.

Aiden moved around the already finished parts of the ballroom, snapping pictures of all the details. He was an exceptionally good photographer, and Deirdre appreciated that he could make all the things she'd brought together look so brilliant.

"The wind is picking up." Meg's voice came through Deirdre's earpiece, and she lifted her head to the wall of glass that took up the back of the ballroom. The beach and bay spread before her there, and sure enough, something tumbled by, fueled by the wind. "She may want to go with the short veil."

Deirdre picked up her phone and spoke into it. "Let's watch it. We still have an hour before she needs to decide that."

Katelin and Hiro had arrived a couple of hours ago and were sequestered upstairs in the bride's and groom's rooms, their friends and family with them as they all got primped and proper for the nuptials. Deirdre looked down at her list and turned her attention to the cake table. The vines and flowers sat there, but no one had touched them yet.

First, she went around and blew out all the candles. The wicks would light better once they'd already burned, but she didn't need them burning for an hour before the event even started. With smoke tendrils lifting into the air, Deirdre walked over to the counter-height table for the cake. Before she could move a single vine, the main entrance opened and someone said, "Cake incoming."

Deirdre swept the live greenery to the back of the table as she stepped around it, pleased as a tall woman came inside, carrying a towering, pristine wedding cake on a cake board. The man held the door, and another woman darted through after the first to help with the board.

"Right here," she called. They came toward her slowly, one step at a time, communicating the whole way.

"All right, Suze," the tall woman—Micah McBride—said. "Get the spatula."

Suze, clearly the other woman, released the board as Micah rested it on the edge of the table. But the man was already there, extending a long pizza oven spatula toward Suze. The two women wore chef's jackets smeared with purple and silver frosting, and Deirdre wondered what time they'd gotten up that morning.

She'd barely been able to sleep, what with this huge wedding today and a beautiful, romantic date with Wyatt last night. He'd been charming and flirtatious at precisely the right moments. Caring and tender after she'd explained the full situation behind Emma's claims. Not that she'd been able to give every single detail. If she had, they'd still be in that booth at The Indian House.

Deirdre had let her emotions get away from her, but Wyatt hadn't seemed like she'd done anything wrong at all. Dalton was forever telling Deirdre not to get so "worked up" about things, and she hadn't spent a lot of her adult years crying over things. Her therapist had told her she had a right to be upset over the lies Emma had told, and that was the first time Deirdre hadn't been ashamed of how she felt.

Last night was another time where she'd felt completely comfortable letting how she truly felt come to the surface. Wyatt hadn't judged her in the slightest, and he'd moved right on to something else without any awkwardness. Deirdre sure did like that about him. She'd worried about a kiss on the way back to her house, but

Wyatt had been nothing but a gentleman as he walked her to her door and hugged her good-night.

Truth be told, Deirdre wouldn't have objected to kissing him. She just wasn't sure if he was ready for that. He'd spoken of his wife several times, and Deirdre liked that he didn't keep Christine in a closet, as if she'd never existed.

"Easy," Micah said as Suze slipped the large pizza spatula under the cake. "There. It's loose." She pulled the board back slightly, and Suze dragged the cake forward. It stopped just short of the middle of the table, but Deirdre was impressed by where they'd managed to get it.

"Micah," she said. "This is simply stunning." The cake spiraled from a wide base up to a tiny layer twelve stories up. The delicate white fondant had been decorated with silver accents and light purple and dark blue flowers. Everything played together remarkably well, and Deirdre remembered the day when Katelin had brought in her rough sketch to meet with Micah.

She'd taken the concept to fruition, and Katelin was going to freak out when she saw it.

"Thanks," Micah said. "You let me know when you have another bride like Katelin. She's been so amazing to work with."

"Isn't she great?" Deirdre would've said that whether Katelin was the biggest Bridezilla or not. Suze got to work fixing the bottom of the cake, and Deirdre started laying the flowers and vines around the cake in the just-right spots.

"Get pictures of this one, Bob," she said. "Have you met my husband?" She beamed at the man and then looked at Deirdre.

"I haven't." Deirdre smiled and shook his hand while Micah introduced her. "Nice to meet you."

"And you." He clicked pictures on his cellphone and stuck it in his back pocket. Suze finally finished up with the frosting and accents she wanted, and then stepped back.

"I'm satisfied."

"Thank goodness," Micah said dryly, and Deirdre giggled at the pair of them. They owned one of the best wedding cakeries in Getaway Bay, and Deirdre had to book six months out to get them. The Cake Walk was a fancy shop too, though they didn't sell from a storefront.

"Thanks, ladies," Deirdre said. "You got the payment yesterday?"

"Yes," Suze said. "It arrived. Thanks so much."

"Thank you," Deirdre said. "You make me look good." She hugged both of the women, and they all left.

Deirdre consulted her list again, her feet beginning to ache. She ignored the pain, because she still had miles to go before she could relax in a bubble bath, a bowl of lemon drops on the edge of the tub and soft music playing from the Bluetooth speaker on her bathroom counter.

She finished the dinner and dancing area and went to

check on her bride. From the second floor, she saw guests starting to arrive, and some of the women were holding their skirts against their legs because of the wind.

After knocking lightly on the bride's door, she said, "Katelin, it's Deirdre." The door opened, and the bride turned toward her. "Oh." Deirdre pressed one hand to her heartbeat, tears pricking her eyes.

Katelin was simply stunning with her hair all curled and pinned up. Her makeup done just right. Her face glowing with love and happiness. All Deirdre could think about was her own daughter and how she might not get to ever experience this with her.

She's only fifteen, she told herself. *There's still time.*

But Deirdre felt like the gulf between her and Emma was as wide as the Pacific Ocean. She could row and row and row and still never get back to her daughter.

She pulled herself together as she hugged Katelin. "The wind is a bit breezy. You might want the shorter veil."

Katelin stepped over to the window and looked outside. "Yep. All right, girls. Short veil."

"Thank all the starfish in the ocean," Katelin's sister said, and a chorus of giggles broke out, Deirdre's included.

DEIRDRE DIDN'T DRAG HERSELF OUT OF BED UNTIL almost ten o'clock the next morning. By the end of the wedding, her back ached, and her feet hurt, and no amount of lavender-scented bubble bath and hot water had helped.

Painkillers had worked their magic, and she'd been watching a show in bed for an hour before she finally swung her legs over the edge of the mattress. Her first thought—after she found some coffee and made toast—was to find out what Wyatt was up to that afternoon. She couldn't imagine a better way to spend a Sunday afternoon than with her hand in his as they walked the beach. A sunset kiss....

Deirdre distracted herself with caffeine and buttery bread, finally pulling out her phone to text Wyatt after she'd put out some cat food for the strays. *What are you doing today? Want to grab some fish tacos and wander the cliffs?*

There was nothing as amazing as the bluffs overlooking the point where Getaway Bay joined East Bay. One of the Your Tidal Forever's wedding planners, Charlotte, lived up on the bluff with her husband, Dawson.

There won't be any people, Deirdre added. *It's private property.*

She didn't particularly like crowds, and she knew Wyatt detested them. He didn't like the scrutiny, and he always wanted to sit with his back to as many people as possible. As if everyone on the island wouldn't know his stature.

"Maybe that's just you," she muttered to herself as she waited for him to reply. He didn't immediately, and she went into her backyard to check on her fruit trees. They'd gotten an insect last spring, and she'd been treating them for months to get rid of the pests.

They seemed to be doing well, and she couldn't wait to have fresh apples, avocados, and limes again.

Her phone chirped, and Deirdre pulled it out of her pocket. *Will we be trespassing? That's a crime, you know.*

Deirdre smiled at her device and quickly tapped the phone icon. She could text him, sure, but it was so much easier to talk, and she was tired.

"You called?" he answered.

Deirdre felt like someone had stuck a light bulb in her mouth and switched it on. If someone could see her now, she supposed she'd look like Katelin had yesterday—glowing and oh-so-happy.

"My friend Charlotte owns the land. She lets us come up there and explore. The view is spectacular, and we can go down some steps to the beach too."

"If I can bring my dog, I'm in," he said. "He's been home alone a lot lately."

"I'm sure you can bring your dog," she said. "What is he again? A German shepherd?"

"He's a mix of some sort," Wyatt said. "His name's Tigger."

"That's right." Deirdre turned back to the house. "Do you want to pick me up in that Jeep of yours about two?"

"Are we eating at two, or going through dinner?"

"Going through dinner," she said. "Is that okay?"

"Of course," he said. "I'm just planning when I can eat next." He chuckled, and Deirdre did too. "Oh, and I have your dishes. I meant to bring them last night, but I forgot."

"It's fine," she said. "See you in a bit."

A couple of hours later, she put a portable battery for her phone in her beach bag and declared herself ready. She'd just opened the front door and stepped onto her porch when Wyatt pulled up in that black Jeep.

He got out though she came down the steps, both of them smiling at one another. "Look at you," he said.

Deirdre did a little twirl for him so her black and floral swimming suit cover-up would flutter around her knees. She laughed at the same time he caught her around the waist, his deeper laugh joining hers.

"And you," she said. "I don't think I've ever seen you wear shorts." And today, he did. Bright, blue and white tribal patterned shorts, paired with a gray T-shirt that had a police badge printed on the front of it.

"Well, you said beach," he said. "And bluffs, so I wore real shoes." He glanced down at her feet. "I see I chose well."

"Nobody ever said you were dumb," she said, and he grinned at her.

Before she knew it, he leaned down and swept his lips across her cheek. "It's great to see you, Deirdre," he said.

Very few people said that to her, and she basked in the warmth moving through her body. "Thanks," she said. "It's good to see you too."

"I can't wait to see what this private property looks like," he said.

Deirdre laughed and shook her hair over her shoulders as they got moving toward the Jeep. "I think you might be disappointed. But let's go."

Chapter Eleven

W yatt didn't think he'd be disappointed by anything that afternoon. He was with Deirdre, and she made everything into an adventure for him. They could literally sit in his Jeep, and he'd be satisfied.

But they were only in the Jeep for about twenty minutes before she directed him to turn left onto a dirt road. "This must be the private property," he said. Sure enough, he spied a bright yellow sign declaring it as such as he passed a fence that looked like it was meant to keep cattle contained. "It's pretty up here."

The ocean was a smear on the horizon, and Wyatt loved the view in that moment. He'd always loved the island, and he'd never wanted to leave to live somewhere else. He'd never seen snow, and he couldn't even imagine what true cold felt like. He had lived through tsunamis and volcanic eruptions and hurricanes. But he'd never wanted to leave Getaway Bay.

"So you can go past the house," Deirdre said. "That's where Charlotte and Dawson live."

Wyatt looked at the stunning house that someone obviously spent a lot of time on. "Charlotte is great," he said. "She did Jen's wedding."

"Oh, oh course." Deirdre scoffed and shook her head. "And here I am talking about her as if you don't know who she is. Sorry."

"It's fine." Wyatt continued down the road, his thoughts wandering to his daughter. "She hasn't called in a while."

"Who?"

"My daughter."

"Park right here," Deirdre said, and Wyatt eased the Jeep to a stop. After getting out, he shouldered a backpack he'd put water and snacks in and took Deirdre's hand.

"How long is a while?" she asked as she led him down a narrow trail and through the rocks. Some of them were definitely the remains of a volcano, and they were beautiful. Plants and shrubs grew anywhere they could, as well as a wildflower Wyatt didn't know the name of.

"A couple of weeks," he said.

"Where is she?"

"Her husband's going to school in California," Wyatt said, and the ocean between him and Jen hadn't bothered him until that moment.

"You have a phone too, Wyatt."

Surprise punched him in the lungs, and he took a breath to try to get the stinging to stop. "You're right," he said. "I do."

"If you want to talk to her, give her a call." Deirdre glanced over at him, and Wyatt felt like a fool. She couldn't call her daughter to talk to her, and he wondered what that could possibly feel like.

Probably a lot like losing his wife, like a piece of herself had died.

He paused, and Deirdre did too. She turned toward him, peering up at him through her sunglasses. "What?"

"Deirdre," he said, his mind misfiring as his mouth turned dry. "I sure do like you."

A smile bloomed on her face, and Wyatt didn't waste another second. He took her into his arms, glad when she came easily. Thrilled that she fit so well. He'd never kissed this woman, and he honestly thought he was about to crash and burn.

Big time.

"I haven't kissed anyone in a long time," he whispered.

"Are you scared?" she asked.

"Terrified," he admitted.

"I'll help you," she said, closing the distance between them, which wasn't much. Wyatt touched his mouth to hers, not quite sure what to expect.

He hadn't known fireworks could explode down his throat, or that his heart could beat that fast and not burst.

He suddenly remembered what to do, and he

growled in the back of his throat when Deirdre pulled away. She didn't go far though, and Wyatt kissed her again easily, everything male in him firing with color and sound and light.

Kissing Deirdre brought new life to his soul, and Wyatt thought that maybe that piece of him that had died was coming back. Growing bigger. Brighter.

He finally pulled away, his head swimming and his chest tight. He pulled in a deep breath as Deirdre tucked herself into his arms. "See?" she murmured. "That was beautiful."

"Beautiful," Wyatt repeated, swaying with her in his arms. Yes, he could get used to afternoons like this, and he hoped he and Deirdre would have many more of them.

———

"There's two tickets to the luau on your desk," Norma said a few days later when Wyatt stopped at her desk for his morning messages. "And I did book that hot air balloon ride over Lobster Bay for you and Deirdre for next weekend." She made a check mark next to something on the notebook in front of her. "And your mother called."

Wyatt finally moved a muscle in his face, and that was to lift his eyebrows. "Must not have been an emergency status call."

"She's heard." Normal adjusted her glasses and set her pencil down.

"Heard what?" Wyatt needed to be in a meeting with his detectives about the shooting-slash-car accident at the business building from last week in five minutes. But his mother calling definitely came first.

"About you and Deirdre," Norma said matter-of-factly. "I calmed her down, which is why this wasn't an emergency." She handed him a piece of paper. "There are the high points. I said you'd call before she went to bed tonight."

Wyatt sighed, though Norma had given him plenty of time to call his mother. "How can she possibly know? We went to dinner one time, on Friday." True, about five days had passed since then, and it was very possible Nita Reddy had seen his mother around the island. Though she was nearing eighty, she didn't let her age stop her from doing anything. Mom did water aerobics every morning at the aquatic center, and she played golf almost every afternoon.

Since Wyatt's father had died a decade ago, she'd determined not to let old age stop her from doing things —and it didn't.

"She would not divulge that information to me." Norma sniffed, which meant his mother had been rude to his secretary.

"I'm sorry for whatever she said, Norma." Wyatt looked at the woman, hoping she knew he meant it.

"I am no stranger to your mother, Wyatt." Normal

put a professional smile on her face. "Now get to your meeting. I don't need to hear how you're late to every-thing and that it's my fault."

"I am not late to everything," he said, rolling his eyes. He did go into his office and set his lunch down on the corner of his desk. His coffee cup landed next, and he peered at the piece of paper with at least a dozen bullet points on it.

The first one said Wants to know why you're dating another blonde.

"This isn't happening," Wyatt grumbled. He crum-pled up the paper and tossed it toward the trash can. It didn't go in, and that was fine with him. He picked up the blue folder Norma had put on his desk and left the office. In the conference room, he sat down at the head of the table and flipped open the folder, just as Noel stood up to start.

He read some of the things as Noel recapped them about the case, but his mind wasn't on topic. Sandi spoke about the ballistics on the bullet casing, and Tom wanted to go over the witness testimonies again. Eli said he'd review Bella's statement, and the one lead they had was a gun shop on the north side of the bay, in a little strip mall before all the ritzy houses started eating their way up the hill.

"Fine," he said. "Noel, you and Sandi go work that lead. Eli, you work with Tom on the statements and testi-monies. I want to see a timeline for this accident or shooting or whatever it was. Where are we with the suspect?"

"We have his statement, and we couldn't charge him with anything."

"He wasn't drunk? High? Outstanding parking ticket?"

"Came back clean, boss. He said a dog ran in front of him, and he swerved to avoid hitting it."

Dubious, for sure, as there was a courtyard between the road and the building, and no indication the driver had hit the brakes at all.

Wyatt sighed and looked around the table. "All right. We need to talk to him again. Let's see if there's something we can get him in here for."

The meeting broke up, and Wyatt took his folder with him. Back in his office, he sat down at his desk and fiddled with the mouse on his computer to get it to wake. Anyone coming in or walking by would think him very seriously studying something crucial online. But really, he had a texting app that he could use on the computer, and he opened a thread to Deirdre.

I have the luau tickets. You still in for tonight?

Wouldn't miss it. Her response came quickly, and Wyatt smiled. He hadn't seen her since Sunday, and he really wanted to hold her hand. Kiss her the way he had up on the bluff. No, the way he had just inside her door after driving her home. Or maybe the way he had as they leaned toward each other over the console in the Jeep.

The bottom line was, he wanted to kiss her again.

Perfect, he sent her. *I'll pick you up at six.*

Deal.

I also have a surprise reservation for next weekend.

A surprise reservation? Isn't that an oxymoron?

He chuckled to himself. *Well, the reservation isn't a surprise. It's what it's for that is.*

So you know, but I don't.

That's how a surprise works.

Deirdre didn't answer for several moments, and Wyatt turned his attention to some real work on his desk. He signed paperwork, so that when Norma marched into his office twenty minutes later, he had everything ready for her.

"Thank you, sir," she said, pivoting to go right back out to her desk. He smiled and shook his head at her. Norma was a real character, and Wyatt sure was lucky to have her. "Wait a second." She paused in the doorway and turned around. Her eyes zeroed in on the wad of paper lying on Wyatt's floor. "Is that the list of things from your mother?"

"No," Wyatt said, practically leaping out of his desk chair. Norma's heels clicked against the industrial tiles, but he managed to get to the paper first. "It's not, Norma." He hid the crumpled paper behind his back. "Go back to your desk."

"Wyatt Gardner," she said. "That was twenty minutes of my morning."

"I'm going to call her," he said. Behind him, his computer bleeped and his phone buzzed on the desktop.

Norma's eyes stayed angry, and now her eyebrow drew down too. "Well, I'll let you get back to your important business, Chief."

He watched her leave this time, relief mingling with the excitement inside him. Deirdre had finally answered with, *Sorry, my boss came in. You better tell me what to expect for the surprise so I wear the right thing.*

A smile filled Wyatt's whole face, and he couldn't wait to take her up in the hot air balloon, the whole world curving before them on all sides.

But he supposed he better call his mother first.

Chapter Twelve

D eirdre pulled up to the police station, her heart
thumping like she'd just run a mile or two. She'd
been to meet with Norma a few times over the past few
weeks. September had turned into October, and while
Deirdre would never call a season winter in Hawaii, it did
get a little cooler.

Wyatt was busy dealing with everything from court
hearings to the big case with the car that had crashed
into the office building to making sure he had enough
officers for the Halloween parade in a couple of weeks.

They'd been out several more times, and Deirdre sure
did like him. Today, she'd asked Norma to be ready to
have people try the food for the department holiday
party. Deirdre circled to the back of the van she'd
borrowed from Your Tidal Forever and opened the doors
to a spread of food she hoped would all get eaten.

She loved crab cakes and profiteroles as much as the

next person, but she lived alone and certainly couldn't eat very many of them. Whatever the men and women here didn't eat, she told herself, she'd take back to Your Tidal Forever.

After hefting one huge, circular tray into her hands, she started for the front doors. She bumped the handicapped button to get the doors to open for her, and her muscles strained as she waited. She hoped Norma had a spot ready for the food.

Sure enough, the woman met her just inside the door. "You should've called me," she said. "You don't need to bring this stuff in. Eli, Wally, go get the food from the back of Deirdre's van."

"Where am I going?" Deirdre asked, about to drop the heavy tray of lobster tails.

"Trey, take that," Norma barked, and a man jumped up from his desk and took the tray from Deirdre.

A sigh passed through her whole body, and she smiled at the officer. "Thank you."

"Over here," Norma said, leading Deirdre through the desks in the room to a long table that had been set up against the back wall. "You tell him where, Deirdre."

"Let's see," she said, thinking through what else she'd picked up. "Let's put the seafood down here." She indicated the right-hand side of the table, and Trey put the lobster down. The crab cakes went beside them, and then the bagel bites with lox and smoked salmon.

"Sandwiches down here," she said as another tray arrived. "And we'll put desserts in the middle." The profiteroles looked divine, and Deirdre smiled fondly at them. She loved delicious food that looked pretty too.

"This looks amazing," Norma said from the end of the table. "Are you sure we can afford this? Seafood is expensive."

"All of this is within your budget," Deirdre said, slipping back into her professional persona. "Now, you can't have it all. That's why we're tasting today." She moved down to the sandwich end of the table. "We have a bacon turkey club, with brown mustard mayo and heirloom tomatoes." The sandwiches were probably four-bites big, and they made Deirdre's mouth water.

"Your second choice is the Kalua pork, with all the traditional Hawaiian spices, with a red cabbage slaw on top. And then we have a fried chicken option, with all-white meat and pickle relish."

In Deirdre's opinion, any of the sandwiches would be amazing. She went through the seafood choices, and then finally, the desserts. "Lemon crème profiteroles," she said. "With a vanilla glaze."

"I don't even know what a profiterole is," Norma said, her pen scratching across her clipboard.

"It's a cream puff," Deirdre said. "Or we can do the doughnut wall we talked about. Or the ice cream sundae bar." She lifted the lids on the few boxes of doughnuts she'd picked up from Nuts About Dough. "They let you pick six varieties," she said. "But I brought their twelve most popular flavors for sampling."

"Wyatt will pick the doughnuts, you just watch,"

Norma said with a sigh. "He loves those breakfast sandwiches with doughnuts for buns."

"You're kidding."

"I wish." Norma laughed then, and Deirdre joined
in. She became aware of Wyatt's presence in the next
moment, and sure enough, she turned to find him
standing only a couple of feet behind her.

"I thought I heard your voice," he said with a smile.

Deirdre wanted to step into his arms and kiss him
hello, the way she'd done a few times now. But she
reminded herself she was at work right now—and so was
he. This wasn't one of their evening dates or weekend
afternoons together. She couldn't kiss him whenever she
wanted, wherever she wanted.

"Hey," she said, smiling at him.

"Is she teasing me?" he asked, lacing his fingers
through hers as he joined her and Norma at the table.

"She said you like those breakfast sandwiches with
doughnuts for buns."

"I totally do," he said. "Ate one yesterday."

Deirdre shook her head. "You're going to have a
heart attack by age fifty."

"I ran five miles this morning," he said. "I think it
evens out, doesn't it?"

Deirdre leaned into him, happier than she'd been in a
very long time. "It probably does."

"Let's gather around," Norma called in a loud voice.
She looked at Deirdre. "We're ready, right?"

"We're ready," she said, falling back a few steps so

Norma could lead the show. She waited while everyone came over to the vicinity of the table. She explained why the food was there and what she wanted from people. She'd made ballots for what type of food they wanted and everything.

"Now," she said, her eyes taking on a fierce quality. "Remember, this is for our Christmas party, and that's going to be a nice affair. *Nice.*" She stepped back and added, "This is Deirdre Bernard, our party planner. I'm going to let her explain the food."

Deirdre smiled out at everyone, though a blip of fear moved through her. So many law enforcement officers and detectives, sergeants, and the Chief of Police himself in one room would've intimidated anyone. At least that was what she told herself.

She explained the food again, just as she had for Norma, and then she got out of the way so people could take the food.

"You're not eating?" Wyatt asked as he joined the line.

"I've tasted all of this food," she said. "If there's some left, I'll have a pork sandwich."

"We can go in my office," he said, picking up a second plate and putting a pork sandwich on it. He took one of everything, and then put a lemon profiterole on her plate too, along with two crab cakes.

Deirdre warmed from the inside. Had she gotten in line and filled her own plate, that was exactly what she would've put on it.

Wyatt carried both of their plates into his office and set hers on the front of his desk while he went around it and sat down.

"Thanks," she said.

He slid a plastic fork across the desk toward her and grinned at her. "I like seeing you here."

"Yeah?" Deirdre didn't think she'd ever get tired of hearing something like that.

"Yeah." Wyatt took a bite of the crispy chicken slider and moaned. "Oh, this is good." He finished it in three bites and wiped his mouth. "The surprise is finally ready."

"Ready?"

"Well, it's happening." He picked up his fork to try the crab cakes. He didn't seem to like those as much as the sandwich options, as he didn't even finish one before turning back to the pork bun. "I just meant, it got postponed a couple of times, and it's finally happening."

"Saturday, right?" Deirdre liked the crab cakes, though they did seem a little dry today.

"Bright and early," he said. "Like, six a.m. early."

Deirdre paused and looked up. "You never said it would be that early."

"I just got a confirmation email." He indicated the computer, as if Deirdre could see it.

"You owe me big time for a Saturday six a.m. wake-up call." She gave him a mock glare and went back to her pork bun. It was tangy and delicious, the slaw adding a crispness and crunch to contrast the meat and soft bread.

Wyatt chuckled and finished his turkey sandwich too. Four bites. "I know. I didn't realize what I'd booked, but the ball—" He cut off, and that made Deirdre look up.

"The what?"

"It's a surprise," he said, a flush working its way into his face. "I almost gave it away." He finished the lobster tail and came back to the last sandwich on his plate. "I think I like the chicken the best."

"It is good," she said, though she hadn't taken one this time. She'd eaten at Crispers plenty of times in the past eighteen months, as a good chicken sandwich was one of her favorite things. "I didn't see you pick up a ballot."

"Oh, right." Wyatt got up and left the office for a moment, closing the door behind him when he returned. Deirdre finished her food as Wyatt marked his choices and handed her the paper.

She stood up to take it, and Wyatt pressed in closer to her. "Wyatt," she whispered. "You're at work."

"Yeah." He took her into his arms. "And I haven't seen you in two days, and the door is closed." He took a deep breath of her hair, which made Deirdre feel cherished.

"Two days," she said, giggling. "You make it sound like years."

"Feels like it," he said just before kissing her. Deirdre

melted into his touch, because she sure did like Wyatt Gardner a whole lot.

"Chief," someone said, and Deirdre shrank against his chest as their kiss broke. He'd hide her behind his body, and maybe she wouldn't have to see who'd walked in on them.

"What?" Wyatt growled, turning to look at whoever stood in his now-open doorway.

"Uh, sorry." The door closed in the next moment, and Wyatt sighed as he looked down at Deirdre. Their eyes met, and Deirdre couldn't help laughing. Wyatt did too, and he stepped back.

"Guess you were right."

"Should've locked that sucker," she said, picking up her paper plate.

"Or stood right in front of it." He followed her to the door and took the plates from her. "Like this." He pressed her into the door and kissed her, and Deirdre lost herself to the passion in his touch. Because, wow. Just wow.

———

Saturday morning, Deirdre woke with excitement bubbling in her stomach. True, it was still plenty dark outside, but the sun would be up soon. Wyatt would be there sooner, and Deirdre hurried to brush her teeth and get dressed. He'd told her to wear something warm, with close-toed shoes and to maybe bring a jacket.

She assumed they'd be doing something outside, and she shimmied into a pair of skinny jeans and put a long-sleeved T-shirt on, and then a zip-up sweatshirt over that. She put on sneakers and had just pulled her hair into a ponytail when Wyatt knocked on the front door.

"I'm coming in," he said in the next moment.

Deirdre called, "I'm almost ready. Be right out," down the hall from her bathroom, and she heard the door close. Wyatt had walked into her house after knocking a few times now, and Deirdre sure did like the familiarity of it. They'd been seeing each other for four weeks now, and this time was completely different than the first time they'd tried a relationship.

Thankfully.

Deirdre had allowed herself to like Wyatt, to kiss him. She wondered as she hurried to swipe on a quick layer of mascara and then lip gloss if she could fall in love with him. Studying her reflection in the mirror, she whispered to herself, "Go find out."

In the living room, Wyatt had found a spot on the end of the couch, and he was frowning at his phone.

"What is it?" she asked.

"Nothing." He got up and pocketed his phone. "A work thing someone else can take care of." He let his eyes slide down her body, and Deirdre did the same to him.

"You look great," she said, the compliment almost sticking in her throat. She wasn't great at validating a man, she knew that. It was one of the things Dalton had told her during the dissolution of their marriage. *You never compliment me. I never know how you feel about me.*

Her throat tightened as she waited for Wyatt to say something. He finally said, "Thanks, sweetheart. So do you." He extended his hand toward her, and Deirdre laced her fingers through his.

He wore jeans too, with a light blue polo with the buttons open at the throat. He smelled like minty toothpaste and musky aftershave, and Deirdre kissed him quickly before he led her to the door with the words, "We really can't be late, or they'll leave without us."

She was dying to know what the surprise was, but she didn't ask. She had—several times—and Wyatt had refused to tell her.

So she'd just be surprised when they showed up wherever he was taking her.

Chapter Thirteen

W yatt pulled into the parking lot at Lobster Bay, the rainbow-colored hot air balloon filling the morning in front of him.

"Wyatt," Deirdre said, her eyes glued to the balloon out the window. "Are we going up in that thing?"

"Yes, ma'am," he said. "Just you and me. A sunrise flight." He opened his door and got out of the car. Deirdre met him at the front of the car before he could go around to open her door.

"This is incredible," she said, her voice awed. The wonder swam in her eyes when she looked at him too, and Wyatt's heart softened for this woman.

"Surprise," he said, taking her hand in his. "Let's go check in with our pilot."

"Is that what they're called? Pilots?"

"I hope so," Wyatt said. "I'm not going up in that thing with just anyone."

Deirdre giggled, and Wyatt wanted to tuck her into his side. Into his life. For good.

The strength of his feelings surprised him, but he also knew they were true. He was in such a better place now, and he'd started to fall in love with Deirdre Bernard. All the way in love.

"Morning," he said to the man standing in the sand, smiling. "I'm Wyatt Gardner. This is Deirdre Bernard. We're your passengers this morning."

"Morning, Chief," the man said, though Wyatt didn't know him. "Deirdre, nice to meet you. I'm Sam Cabelli, your balloon pilot this morning."

Wyatt and Deirdre exchanged a glance, both of them grinning.

"There are some safety rules for our flight," Sam said. "So if you'll step up into the basket, we'll go over those before we leave the ground."

Wyatt steadied Deirdre as she climbed in first. "Oh, my," she said, a shaky laugh following. "It's more stable than I thought it would be."

He joined her, with Sam bringing up the rear and securing the latch on the gate behind him. "Okay," he said. "First rule: there are no sudden movements in the basket. Second, no leaning over. Third, you don't touch anything." He smiled through it all, though Wyatt had the feeling he was being very serious.

"Basically, your job is to enjoy yourselves," he said. "I've got hot chocolate or coffee, as well as doughnuts or danishes."

Deirdre looked at Wyatt, and he knew which he wanted. He couldn't help his love of doughnuts, and while he hadn't gotten up to work out this morning, there was always tomorrow. He tucked Deirdre into his side and faced Sam again.

"We'll pass out the food once we get to our maximum height, which is twelve hundred feet. We'll—"

"Twelve *hundred* feet?" Deirdre asked, obviously alarmed. She looked from Wyatt to Sam, who simply kept smiling.

"That's right," he said. "You'll have a three-hundred-sixty-degree view of the islands and the ocean. It's truly spectacular."

"Twelve hundred feet," she repeated.

Wyatt chuckled and pulled her a little closer, though she was right at his side.

"We'll be up at that altitude for about forty minutes," Sam said. "Then we'll gradually descend. I should have you back on the ground in about ninety minutes. You can ask any questions you want while we're up there, and all of the food on-board is for the two of you. This is your flight. I hope you enjoy it." He turned to attend to the controls, talking about what the basket and balloon were made out of, and the fact that hot air balloons actually had holes at the top and bottom of the nylon.

"Holes," Deirdre muttered, and Wyatt could admit that his own nerves were screaming a warning at him.

Then Sam turned on the flame, and a roar filled the

space around them. Fire shot upward, putting that hot air into the nylon. And the balloon began to rise.

"What are we doing?" Deirdre asked, her tone near panic now. "Wyatt, this is insane."

"Hold on," he said, glad there were handholds along the edge of the basket. He wasn't sure he was standing on solid ground either, but Sam guided the balloon smoothly up. And up. And up.

"Wow," Wyatt murmured as his view of the horizon expanded. He twisted slightly, not wanting to move too much in case it dislodged the balloon's flight path, and looked over the island of Getaway Bay.

They were rising fast now that he had landmarks to use, and he easily picked out the station along the biggest road running east and west across the island.

"This is incredible," he said. "Are you looking at the island, Deirdre?"

"I'm afraid to move," she said.

"You can move freely," Sam said. "Don't worry about that. There's hardly a breeze this morning, too, which is nice."

Wyatt couldn't even imagine being in a balloon in some of the wind the island experienced, and he was suddenly glad this excursion had been cancelled the past two weekends due to wind. He'd been disappointed then, but now, he knew how important the weather conditions needed to be.

"I feel like I need to be strapped in," Deirdre said,

but she managed to edge around Wyatt so she could see the island. "Wow."

Wyatt had already said that, but she was absolutely right. The ocean seemed flat and dark. The greens on the trees were vibrant and alive, with the white slashes for the beaches surrounding everything.

He put his arm around Deirdre's waist, and she leaned into him. Powerful feelings moved through him then, and he pressed a kiss to her temple. "There is no one I'd rather experience this with than you," he whispered.

Deirdre's only response was to press further into him, making Wyatt feel like the luckiest man in the world.

"Okay," Sam said a few minutes later. "We just passed one thousand feet."

"I can't look down," Deirdre said.

Wyatt didn't want to either, and he said, "Just keep your eyes out on the horizon."

"We'll move around all three bays," Sam said. "And then make our way back here over the rain forested parts of the island."

Wyatt enjoyed the silence, punctuated by bursts of hot air as Sam piloted them along a route only he knew. Wyatt drank in the spirit of the ocean, the peace of the island, and the joy of being with Deirdre.

"Doughnuts?" Sam asked, and that was literally the only thing that could've made this morning better. He ate an apple and mango fritter as the sun finally lifted itself out of the ocean, casting a new glow over the scene.

Deirdre sucked in a breath and said, "This is incredible." She gazed up at Wyatt. "Thank you, Wyatt. This is the best surprise I've ever gotten." She tipped up to kiss him, and Wyatt couldn't think of a better way to spend his morning. Any morning.

They took pictures and drank their way through the coffee and hot chocolate and ate pastries. Deirdre asked Sam questions, and Wyatt listened to the sound of her voice. By the time they touched down very close to where they'd taken off, Wyatt had a very strong feeling that he'd just fallen all the way in love with Deirdre Bernard.

They stayed to watch Sam take down the balloon completely, and then Wyatt walked with Deirdre down the beach, their shoes discarded near the front bumper of his Jeep.

Deirdre seemed content with her own thoughts, and Wyatt couldn't think of anything to say that didn't start and end with *I love you*. He didn't think she was ready to hear those words—and honestly, he wasn't ready to say them.

Up in the air, everything had been clear. Down on the ground, though, he wondered if a month was enough time to really be in love. Maybe he'd just experienced some of the magic of the morning. Either way, he didn't think Deirdre was going anywhere, and they'd hopefully have plenty of experiences that could testify to him and let him know if how he felt right now was really true.

"I need to sit for a second," she said, and she lowered

herself onto the sand with a sigh. "That was a lot of standing. Worth it, but a lot of standing."

Wyatt groaned as he sat beside her, the sand soft beneath him. "Agreed."

"I didn't even know Lobster Bay was a thing," she said, lacing her arm through his and leaning her head against his bicep.

"It's really just this," he said. "It's not like East Bay or Getaway Bay, with huge beaches and hotels and stuff. This is the best snorkeling on the island though."

"Why isn't anyone here then?" she asked.

"So we can have privacy for this." He turned toward her and kissed her, thrilled when her fingers moved into his hair. He laid her down on the sand and kept kissing her, feeling thirty years younger as he made out with his girlfriend on the beach.

And the best part? There wasn't anyone to interrupt him with the word, "Chief?" No distractions. Nothing but him and Deirdre, as he tried to tell her he loved her without using a single word.

———

A WEEK PASSED, THEN TWO. THE HALLOWEEN PARADE WAS in just one more day, and Wyatt would be glad when it was over. Most people probably didn't know that Halloween was one of the most stressful days for a police officer.

All that makeup, all the masks, and hats, and flowing

costumes. It made identifying threats terribly difficult, and Wyatt didn't want anyone on the island to get hurt. More kids got lost on Halloween in Getaway Bay than any other time of year, and he couldn't wait until Wednesday, when it would all be behind him for another year.

Today, he had a meeting over near Deirdre, and he'd said he'd stop by her office and take her to lunch. They'd planned to simply walk down the boardwalk to Manny's and get tacos. Easy things like that made Wyatt's heart sing as loudly as the bigger dates they'd had.

He'd taken her to movies, on a couple of hikes with him and Tigger, and they had plans to go snorkeling that weekend. He saw her almost every day, but they both had schedules and very full jobs, so there were times where two or three days would pass with only calls or texts.

Wyatt was fine with all of it. He didn't need to move quickly, not when he could take her hand and hold it whenever he wanted. Kiss her hello and goodbye and everything in between. Call or text at any hour.

He flipped a black ballpoint pen from one hand to the next as he listened to a lecture from a K9 sergeant from another island department talk about the dogs he'd been training. Wyatt had wanted to bring in a K9 unit for years, and it was finally going to happen—but through the Sheriff's department.

That was fine with Wyatt, and he'd been working closely with Sheriff Tracey Batista, who'd be the one to monitor the dogs and the men who worked with them.

The meeting finally ended, and Wyatt stood up. His uniform itched along the collar, but he didn't move to scratch his skin. He shook hands with everyone, thanked them for coming from Oahu, and headed out to his cruiser.

Your Tidal Forever sat just down the street, and he arrived before his air conditioning had truly cooled the air inside his car. The scent of frosting and flowers met his nose when he entered the building, and he took a moment to remember the last time he'd been here.

Jen had wanted—and gotten—a big Getaway Bay-wide celebration for her wedding. Wyatt had come to almost every appointment here with her to make sure she got the dress she wanted. The food. The decorations. The invitations. All of it. Your Tidal Forever could handle as little or as much as a bride wanted, and Jen had wanted it all.

"Morning, Chief," someone chirped, and he looked to the smiling woman several feet in front of him, standing behind a desk. Sunny, the receptionist. "Are you here for Deirdre?"

"Yes, please," he said. "But I can go back to her office, can't I?"

"She's in a meeting," Sunny said. "Can I get you a bottle of water? Coffee? I just heard that they'll be done in ten minutes." She kept her smile perfectly in place, and Wyatt thought she put off good energy.

"Water is fine," he said as his phone buzzed. He

pulled it from his pocket to find Deirdre had texted to say *Ten min. Sorry.*

No problem, he sent back.

"Here you go, Chief." Sunny held a bottle of water toward him, and he took it from her.

"Thank you." He sat on the couch and started thumbing through his phone. His email would be a nightmare by the time he got back to his office, and he tapped to read the important ones from Norma.

His heart thumped out a couple of extra beats when he got to the message about finding the driver of the car that had crashed into the office building in a known drug area and being able to arrest him for possession.

What's going on with Villalobos? He typed quickly and sent the text to his lead detective on the case, Noel.

Just got him back to the station. Want us to wait to question him until you get here?

Wyatt looked up as if Deirdre would be right there. She wasn't, as only a couple of minutes had passed since she'd said she needed ten. He didn't want to cancel their lunch, but he did think he should be there for the interrogation of the only lead they had in the shooting case.

Give me a few minutes, he sent to Noel. *Set him up nice and comfortable, and I'll be there in half an hour.* That would give him time to talk to Deirdre, not just leave and text her later.

A few minutes later, the door to his left opened, and a whole group of women spilled out of it. He knew most of them, as they worked here and he'd been here numerous times before. They didn't all scatter to their offices, and Wyatt stood to find Deirdre.

She came toward him. "Uh oh," she said. "You have that look on your face."

"We have a suspect in custody I need to speak with."

Disappointment flashed in her eyes, and Wyatt felt it keenly in his gut. "Okay," she said. "Go."

"I'm sorry," he said. He really didn't want to disappoint her. They'd had dozens of good dates that he hadn't broken. Lots of commitments he'd kept. "Wouldn't you want to talk to Emma if you could?"

She sucked in a breath, pure shock covering every other emotion in her eyes. She crossed her arms and looked around at the same time Wyatt realized he'd made a mistake.

"I'm—"

"I said it was fine," she said, her voice on the icy side. "I'll talk to you later." She turned away from him then, and Wyatt felt her receding from him the way the waves pulled back from the shore.

His phone rang then, and Noel's name sat on the screen. He wanted to make things right with Deirdre before he left. He hated to leave her when she was upset, and he cursed himself for mentioning her daughter.

The daughter she hadn't spoken with in a very long time. That she *couldn't* speak with.

"I'm sorry," he said, finishing what he'd started to say earlier. Deirdre's shoulders barely moved, and he swiped on the call from Noel.

"Chief," Noel said, and Wyatt thought once again about retiring.

"Yep," he said. "I'm on my way." And with that, he walked out of Your Tidal Forever, but hopefully not out of Deirdre's life.

Chapter Fourteen

Deirdre felt cold from head to toe, though the air conditioner in the building had actually been on the fritz and it was hotter than normal. Charlotte's office had almost been insufferable with all the bodies in there and so many decisions being discussed to death.

But her bride had some very specific requests, and Deirdre felt it best to get everyone's opinion on them.

"Thank you so much," Michelle said, stepping over to Deirdre and hugging her.

"Oh, you're welcome," she said, patting her bride on the back. Her heart still wasn't sure how to beat normally after Wyatt had said her daughter's name right out loud for everyone to hear.

The woman stepped back and joined her mother, and they smiled around at all the wedding planners. Charlotte's expertise had been crucial, and Deirdre was glad she'd asked her friend for help. She also had a delicate way of explaining why certain things wouldn't work, and they'd managed to get Michelle away from the idea of a wedding location up in the mountains.

Guests simply wouldn't be able to attend, Charlotte had said. Deirdre had said the same thing, but in a different way. Charlotte made things personal, asking Michelle about her grandmother and disabled aunt, and Michelle had come to the conclusion herself that the mountain locale wouldn't work.

"So who's Emma?" Michelle asked.

"Oh, uh...." Deirdre didn't know how to answer. Could she lie? She'd only told one person at Your Tidal Forever about Emma, and that was Lisa. The other wedding planner caught Deirdre's eye, and she must have had panic in her expression, because Lisa came right toward her.

"Hey, Michelle," she said, pure professionalism in her voice. "I can't wait to see that dress on you." She guided them toward the door, and Michelle and her mother left. Lisa returned to her and asked, "What's going on?"

Tears filled Deirdre's eyes, and she couldn't speak.

"Did she cancel?" Lisa gestured for the other women to come over, but that was the last thing Deirdre wanted. "It's going to be okay."

"What's wrong?" Charlotte asked, touching Deirdre's shoulder.

Deirdre didn't know what to tell them.

"Is it something with Wyatt?" Meg asked. "Maybe we should go back in your office, Charlotte."

"Yes," Lisa said. "Come on. Shannon, grab some water, would you?"

Deirdre went with her friends when she wanted to flee. What was she going to tell them? Activity flurried around her, and Deirdre allowed Lisa to guide her back into the office. Shannon's heels clicked into the room a moment later, and the door closed behind her.

She sat down, and she was very aware of all the eyes on her. Even two was too many, and Deirdre covered her face. She didn't want to expose all of her secrets, and how dare Wyatt say anything about her daughter?

In front of a client, no less.

"Deirdre?" Lisa asked, her voice timid.

Deirdre drew in a deep breath and let her anger take over. That way, she wouldn't cry. That way, she wouldn't come off as pathetic. Just having the protective order was pathetic enough.

"Wyatt was going to take me to lunch," she said. "But he got a call for work, and I was disappointed." She looked around at the other women. They were all professionals, put together with slacks and skirts and earrings. She knew them, but she didn't *know* them. Meg and Lisa knew the most about her, and Deirdre simply had a hard time making friends. Not one of them knew about the protective order.

"To help me see what he needed to do and why," she said, "He mentioned my daughter. And Michelle overheard and asked me who Emma was." Her chin started to tremble, and Deirdre sucked in a tight breath.

Then another, and another. "I didn't know what to say."

Charlotte and Shannon exchanged a glance, and Lisa's eyes widened. "What did you tell her?" Lisa asked.

"Nothing," Deirdre said. "You came over and saved me."

Lisa gave her a sympathetic smile and moved to hug her.

"I didn't know you had a daughter," Meg said, and Deirdre looked at her as Lisa backed up.

"Neither did I," Charlotte said.

"Only Lisa knows," Deirdre said. She ducked her head and studied her hands. "And even she doesn't know the whole story."

The very room itself held its breath, waiting for Deirdre to continue.

"My daughter is fifteen," Deirdre said, deciding to go with the surface level stuff. "She lives with my ex-husband on the North Shore. I came here after a judge granted her a protective order against me. I haven't spoken to her in almost nineteen months."

She looked up then, the surprise, shock, and horror on the women's faces in the room not hard to find. Her stomach tightened and rioted, and Deirdre needed to get out of this room. She just had one more thing to say.

"It's a civil matter," she said. "I'm not a criminal. But I can't talk to my daughter, and Wyatt basically just threw it in my face." She got up, her feet feeling like someone had encased them in cement. They tingled, and she looked down at the floor.

"What are you going to do?" Lisa asked.

"Do?" Deirdre asked. "I'm going to go get to work on what we decided in that meeting. Michelle is a great girl, but she's got opinions, and she wants the perfect wedding. I want to give her the perfect wedding."

With that, Deirdre left the four of them in Charlotte's office. Let them talk. Speculate. Whatever they wanted. She didn't owe them more than what she'd told them, and she had a ton of work to do.

Back in her own office, she closed and locked the door, switched off the lights, and sat heavily in her desk chair. She didn't mean to shut everyone out of her life. It was just easier that way.

She'd been doing so great in Getaway Bay too. She'd been making friends here at work. Maybe it took longer for her to really trust and open up to other women, but she'd been doing it. She'd been seeing Wyatt for just over six weeks, and that topped their last try at a relationship. Why had he said that?

Her phone chimed, and she looked at it out of instinct when she really wanted to ignore it.

Meg's name flashed across the top of the screen, and Deirdre flipped her phone over. The notifications just kept coming, and she hurried to silence the phone and then put it face-down. Then, finally, she could breathe. She could work. She had peace.

———

Deirdre had just finished a pint of lemon sorbet—the only thing she'd had in her freezer—when someone knocked on her front door. She froze with the spoon in mid-air, knowing that knock.

Wyatt may have called or texted—or both—at some point that day. Deirdre didn't know. She'd turned her phone off before leaving the office, and it currently sat in her bedroom, plugged in on the nightstand.

"Deirdre?" he called, and that unlocked the trance she'd fallen into. She bolted to her feet and went straight to the door, not bothering to take the sorbet container into the kitchen.

Her heart thrashed in her chest, and she wanted to tell Wyatt to go away. But they were adults, and adults didn't shout through closed doors if they wanted to solve a problem. So she unlatched the chain and twisted the lock to open the door.

Their eyes met, and Deirdre's anger grew with every second he remained silent. After what felt like a long time, she asked, "You came to my house. Was there something you needed?"

He blinked and cleared his throat. "Yes," he said. "I realize I made a mistake today, and I wanted to apologize." His eyes dropped to the empty sorbet container, and Deirdre had the sudden urge to hide it behind her back.

She did, embarrassment coiling through her. It didn't

play well with the anger, but Deirdre didn't know what to do with anything she was feeling.

"No one's heard from you," he said.

"Who have you been talking to?" she demanded. She didn't need her friends gossiping behind her back.

He looked puzzled, his eyes darkening. "Just Norma," he said. "In a desperate attempt to get you on the phone, I had her call you, thinking you'd answer a call from a client."

Thunder rolled through the sky overhead, and Wyatt looked up.

"You better come in," Deirdre said. "And all the kids better start praying that storm blows over before tomorrow."

"And all my officers," Wyatt said darkly, coming into her house.

She took the empty carton into the kitchen and threw it away, putting the island and couch between her and Wyatt.

"I'm sorry," he said again.

"You've said that," she said. "What I want to know is *what* you're sorry for." She folded her arms, because it was barely seven o'clock and she'd been in her pajamas since the moment she'd gotten home from work.

Wyatt still wore his uniform, and he looked one breath away from passing out. "Running out on you today," he said, and Deirdre shook her head. "And mentioning Emma." He hung his head. "I realize I shouldn't have done that."

"No," Deirdre bit out. "You shouldn't have." She drew in a deep breath, about to let him have it. "You realize that only two people in this entire town know about Emma? You and Lisa Ashford. Lewiston. Whatever."

"I didn't know that."

"Two people, Wyatt. *Two*. And because of you, I had to tell all the girls at work, and they all looked at me like I'm some kind of monster." Her chest heaved and she felt wild and reckless. "What you did is not fair."

"I'm sorry," he said again, lifting his eyes to hers. "But Deirdre, you don't need to be embarrassed about this."

"Don't tell me how to feel."

"You need to trust people more," he said, clearly angry too. "Last time we dated, you accused *me* of not being ready. Of not being willing to open up. Deirdre, that's *you*. With *everyone*." He drew in a deep breath and shook his head. "I didn't come here to argue." He stuffed his hands in his pockets. "I came to apologize and make sure you were okay."

"I'm fine," she snapped.

Wyatt held her gaze, and his was so intense and so deep that Deirdre looked away after only a few seconds. No wonder he was a very good police officer. A look like that could draw a confession out of anyone.

The tension in the air choked her, and she hated feeling like this. She'd had enough of the stress unsettling her stomach. Enough of the worry gnawing at her nerves night and day.

"Deirdre," Wyatt said quietly, and she lost the battle against the tears. They burned in her eyes, and she swiped at her right one quickly.

"I'm fine," she said again, much softer now. "Thank you for checking on me."

"Are we still on for Bora Bora's tomorrow night? I have a reservation."

"Yes," she said.

"All right." Wyatt took a breath and pushed the air out of his mouth loudly. He came toward her, and Deirdre looked up at him for a split second before he gathered her into his arms. "I'm sorry, sweetheart."

"I know." She clung to him, because it was nice to not have to be so strong, so stoic, all the time. She needed someone she could be vulnerable with, and maybe—just maybe—he was right. She didn't open up to very many people, and she needed a shoulder to cry on sometimes. Everyone did, didn't they?

He pressed his lips to her forehead and held her tight. "Okay, well, I'm beat, and my neighbor has called me twice about my dog. I better go."

"Thanks for stopping by." Deirdre walked him to the door and held it while he went out onto her porch. He turned back and lifted his hand in a wave before going down the few steps to his cruiser.

She watched him back out and drive down the lane with palms and banyans swaying in the wind all around her. Then she shut the storm out, wishing the one inside her heart would blow itself out by morning too.

But Deirdre knew better than most that wishing something to be true almost never made it so, and she sighed as she went back to the couch and collapsed onto it. "Sure wish I had more lemon sorbet," she murmured. But she didn't, and no amount of wishing would make some appear, just like wishing for Emma to talk to her had never happened.

Chapter Fifteen

W yatt stood outside the interrogation room while Noel and Tom spoke with Stephen Villalobos, the man who'd been driving the car when it went into the building. This was the third interview in as many days, and Wyatt was weary of the man's lies.

Tom and Noel had run down one of the people Villalobos had identified yesterday, and the two stories didn't match up. Wyatt just needed Villalobos to confess.

"Mister Villalobos," Noel said, unbuttoning his jacket as he sat down. "We talked to the owner at the diner on Palm. He said you were there with Bella. Several times." Tom sat too, slower, and with his eyes never leaving the suspect's.

"Tell us what happened with her," Tom said.

"I've told you already," Stephen said. "We were just friends."

"Why'd you drive into the building?"

"There was a dog, and I swerved to miss it, and after that, the car just went crazy."

He'd been saying that since the beginning, though no one had seen a dog at the scene. Wyatt also needed the report back on the vehicle to see if something had been sabotaged or wrong with the car while Stephen was driving it. He couldn't imagine that to be the case, but he wasn't one to make conclusions without facts. Even then, he liked to think through every scenario. There was nothing more dangerous than thinking he knew the answer to something without doing the work.

The interview continued, but it wasn't anything new. Wyatt retreated to the back wall and leaned against it, keeping one ear on the conversation but really, his mind had moved on to another problem.

Deirdre.

And he hated categorizing her as a problem. He was the one that had blown things up between them, but she was the one who wasn't ready this time. She'd all but admitted it a couple of nights ago when he'd stopped by her house.

They'd gone to Bora Bora's last night, but the tension between them had been sky-high, and Wyatt hadn't known how to break it. He had no plans to see her that evening, and neither of them had texted that day either.

Wyatt had been trying to think of something they could talk about. Something to bring them together again. He picked up his phone and tapped a few times to get to their text string.

He had something he could tell her, but he didn't want to do it over text. He liked the ease of modern technology, and how it made detective work easier, opened up new avenues for cold cases, and made communication faster.

But he thought it also made things less personal. And Wyatt wanted personal with Deirdre.

Lunch today?

He sent the text before he could change his mind.

The door to the interrogation room opened, and Tom and Noel came out. "Sorry, Chief," Noel said.

"Lawyer?" Wyatt asked.

"Yep." Tom nodded as he went past.

"Let's keep him as long as we can," Wyatt said. "Does he have a name for us?"

"Nope." Noel handed him the case file, but Wyatt didn't open it. The detective secretary would call for a public defender, and they could take hours to show up. Maybe Mr. Villalobos would feel like talking then.

Wyatt went back to his office, catching sight of Norma arranging a new vase of flowers on her desk. "Who's that from?" he asked. "Rick?"

"That's right." His secretary beamed at him. "It's our anniversary next week."

"So he started early."

"He'll do something every day this month," Norma said. "It's our anniversary month." She finished with the last lily and sat down. "The Harrison kid was found," she said. "The mother called in a few minutes ago."

143

"Good news," Wyatt said. He'd survived Halloween with only two missing children reports, and they were both accounted for now. And there hadn't been any incidents during the parade, and he had officers out all over the bays to make sure yards and streets were clean or getting cleaned up.

Wyatt hated Halloween, and he went into his office and closed the door. He didn't like how every little stressor at work bothered him when he wasn't happy in his personal life. The past several weeks with Deirdre had made the job easier, that was for sure, and he practically lunged for his phone when it chimed.

Sure, Deirdre had said. *And I need to meet with Norma this afternoon, so you could give me a ride.*

Sounds good. Wyatt leaned back in his chair, satisfied that they'd had a normal conversation. He managed to get some work done, emails answered, and new cases assigned before he left for lunch.

Deirdre had already arrived at Mama Chu's when Wyatt got there, and he leaned down and kissed her quickly as he joined her at the table. "Hey," he said, smiling. "It's great to see you."

She didn't seem as withdrawn today as she had yesterday, and Wyatt was counting that as a win. "You too."

"My mother asked about Thanksgiving again," he said, picking up the menu. "What do you think?" He'd asked her to go to Thanksgiving dinner with him, at his mother's place. His two siblings would be there too, and she wanted to have a full house. Since Christine's death, Wyatt had been spending all major holidays with his mother, and he wasn't sure what to tell her. Deirdre didn't have any family she could visit, and he'd invited her to spend the holidays with his.

Deirdre had said she wanted to think about it, and that was before what had happened at Your Tidal Forever a couple of days ago.

"Yeah," Deirdre said, giving him a smile. "We can go."

Relief spread through Wyatt, but he didn't feel quite out of the woods yet. "Great." He looked up as the waitress approached. They put in their orders, and Wyatt looked at Deirdre again. "I have something I want to talk with you about."

"Oh?"

"Yeah." Wyatt studied the table for a moment. "I'm thinking about retiring." He looked up, feeling a mixture of things. Selfish. Vulnerable. Like he could really use a friend.

"Wow, really?" Deirdre reached across the table and took one of his hands in both of hers. Wyatt further relaxed with her touch. Maybe they really were okay. "Do you not like your job?"

"I like it," he said. "I've loved it. I just think it might be time."

"And what are you going to do?" she asked. "You're not even forty-five years old yet."

"I haven't thought that far ahead."

"Can you go back to being a detective? Do you have to be the Chief of Police?"

"I mean, people don't usually go backward," he said. "I don't know. Maybe I just need a vacation. Maybe I'm fine."

Deirdre cocked her head, studying him. He liked that she thought about things. That she didn't just try to talk him out of it or accept what he said. "Maybe it's something to think about," she said. "Do you get a pension with the years you've put in?"

"Yes," he said. "I have twenty-three with the state. I get a pension with that. And I can work somewhere else too, adding years as long as it's within the state retirement system."

"Like what?" She reached for her soda the moment the waitress set it on the table. Wyatt did too, taking his time as he unwrapped the straw and put it in his diet cola.

"Public school," he said. "The state university. Prison system. Anything like that."

"Prison system. Wow." Deirdre looked at him with questions in her eyes.

"I don't want to work in the prison system," he said. "But maybe I could teach at the university or something. Criminal justice. Criminology. Law enforcement management. That type of thing."

"Sounds like you have a lot of questions to ask someone," she said.

"Yeah," Wyatt said. "Anyway." He blew out his breath. "What's new with you? How's your new bride?"

"Oh, she's…." Deirdre laughed, and Wyatt felt even more tension bleed out of the air around them. "She's excitable. She's been saving for three years to hire us, and I sure hope I can give her what she's dreamed of." She glanced up as the food arrived, and their conversation lulled again.

"Excitable." Wyatt chuckled and picked up his fork. "And what are you doing with Norma this afternoon?"

"Décor," she said.

"Oh, boy," Wyatt said. "Well, come see me if you have a minute." He met her eye, and he had so much he wanted to say to her. "Okay?"

Deirdre smiled and ducked her head, and Wyatt thought they were going to be okay. "Okay."

———

THE WEEKS PASSED, AND NORMA GOT CANDY OR JEWELRY or lunch or flowers every day in November, true to her word about her husband making it their anniversary month. Wyatt was tired just looking at all the gifts as they came in, and he couldn't imagine planning something like that.

He and Deirdre seemed to be moving along, maybe at a slower pace than before, but things felt normal to Wyatt when they were together. She held his hand. She kissed him with the same passion as previously. They laughed together. They hiked though the weather was cooling and it rained sometimes.

Wyatt pulled up to her house on Thanksgiving Day morning, the sun shining though the air held a crispness now that it was almost December. He climbed the steps, but Deirdre came out before he could knock. She wore a dress that hung down to her knees and showed her legs, and Wyatt's mouth went dry.

"Wow," he said. "You look great."

"Thank you." She reached out and touched the top button on his shirt. Fire spread down his chest at the warmth in her fingers, but he didn't move. "Is this a new shirt?"

"Yes," he said. "I always wear a new shirt to my mother's. Then I know it's clean."

Deirdre laughed, but Wyatt wasn't kidding. "My mother, she's...."

"You've told me about her," Deirdre said. "I can handle it. I work with brides-to-be for a living." She laughed. "Most of them are great," she said. "So great. But I can handle a...prickly personality."

"Let's hit the road then. It's over on the west side of the island, about an hour away."

"All right, Chief." She gave him a flirtatious grin and went down the steps. She could get in the Jeep herself, but Wyatt liked to be a gentleman and help her. Plus, that meant he got to stand close to her, smell that fruity perfume.

He closed her door and rounded the vehicle, taking a

deep breath of the rain forest air. "You live on a beautiful part of the island," he said as he climbed in.

"I agree," she said. "The beach has its place, but I love being up in the trees more."

Wyatt got them on the road, and they chatted about his daughter and her plans for the holidays as they drove the coastal highway. "The whales are back," he said, turning the conversation to something else. "Have you been out on the speedboats to see them?"

"I didn't even know that was a thing."

"Oh, it's a thing, and you can see some amazing animals," he said. "I saw a blue whale shoot right out of the water last year." He glanced at her. "Do you want to go?"

"Absolutely."

"It's quite the speedboat ride," he said. "About five miles off the coast, at forty miles per hour."

"So don't do my hair," she said. "Got it."

Wyatt chuckled, so happy to be in the car with her. Celebrating the holidays with her. He wasn't alone for the first time in four years, and it felt fantastic. He finally pulled up to a house that sat only half a block from the beach, and the sand seemed to have crowded its way all the way to his mother's front porch.

"Here we are." He peered out the windshield at the white house with green shutters and a matching green door.

"Did you grow up here?" she asked.

"No, Mom moved here after my dad died. They lived

149

in Getaway Bay. I grew up there." He looked at her. "You ready for this? I can practically hear the noise from here."

"Two siblings," she said. "A sister and a brother. With teenagers."

"Loud teenagers," he said, opening his door. "And the badge does nothing to quiet them."

Deirdre laughed and joined him at the front of the Jeep. Melinda's car was already in front of the house, as was Scott's. So they were the last to arrive, and Wyatt would probably hear about that for the next year.

He opened the door and yelled, "We're here," over the noise at the same time he reached for Deirdre's hand. All sound silenced, and Wyatt marveled at it. So that was how it was done.

Bring a woman home for Thanksgiving, and he'd get some peace and quiet.

Chapter Sixteen

Deirdre felt the weight of almost a dozen pairs of eyes on her. Even Wyatt was looking at her, and she suddenly had the urge to run to a bathroom and check her reflection. But she'd done that at least ten times before Wyatt had arrived at her house.

Her hair was perfectly curled and fell over her shoulders in blonde waves. She wore makeup, but not too much. Tasteful makeup. She'd put on a dress, which was a huge tell for how much she liked Wyatt and wanted to impress his family.

But the truth was, families were not something Deirdre was very good with. She'd ruined her relationship with her mother because of her devotion to Dalton, following him all over the country, moving every time he got a little too friendly with a woman in his office.

And of course, it wasn't like she spoke to her ex or her own daughter anymore. She barely knew how to act at functions like this, as she hadn't been to a large family meal like this in at least a decade. Maybe longer.

Her nerves, which had been fluttering all morning, now flapped like eagle's wings. She couldn't quite get a decent breath, especially not when Wyatt said, "Hey, everyone. This is Deirdre Bernard, my girlfriend."

"Look at you," the man said—Scott, Wyatt's brother. He grinned at Wyatt and then Deirdre. "She's really pretty, Wyatt." He embraced Wyatt as they laughed, and then Scott extended his hand to Deirdre.

"My brother, Scott," Wyatt said needlessly. They'd gone over his family. Scott had a wife named Amelia, with two teenage girls, Kiley and Brinley.

She said hello to all of them, smiling and shaking hands, until she'd met his sister and her husband too. Joan and Aaron, with a boy and two girls.

"My mother, Laura." Wyatt put his arm around his mother's shoulders and faced Deirdre, both of them smiling.

"You're just lovely," Laura said. "Welcome." She hugged Deirdre, who leaned into the elderly woman's embrace and held on. It sure did feel nice—and it also reminded Deirdre of what she would never have.

Her lungs pinched, and her heartbeat accelerated. But she kept her smile on her face as her other senses started to function properly. "Smells great in here," she said, getting a hint of sage and fresh bread hidden beneath the roasted turkey scent.

"Joan's been cooking for hours," Laura said.

"I thought we weren't eating until two," Wyatt said.

"We aren't," his sister said, putting a vegetable platter on the table in front of her kids. "We're making our own placemats and having appetizers."

Deirdre had no desire to make her own placemat, but she sat down at an empty spot at the table, Wyatt at her side. She stared at the art supplies on the table, wondering if this was what normal families did.

"After this," Carina said, looking at Deirdre. "She makes us play board games. Take your time."

Deirdre couldn't help the giggle that came out of her mouth, though she ached for an afternoon like this with Emma. Making placemats as they ate carrots and ranch dressing. Playing a board game as they laughed and made memories.

Her throat closed, and she stood up.

"Deirdre?" Wyatt asked.

"Restroom?" she asked, because she had to get out of there. Just for a minute. Just to clear her head and stop thinking about what might've been.

"Oh, it's down the hall," Amelia said, putting a bowl of salsa on the table and dropping a bag of chips next to it. Deirdre didn't see how she'd be hungry for a huge meal in only a few hours with the amount of food that was already on the table. "Third door on your right."

Deirdre gave her a tight smile and practically ran away. Behind the closed and locked door of the bathroom, she pressed her back into the wood and breathed.

Her skin felt clammy, and she wiped her forehead and found it sweaty.

Her hands shook, but that subsided quickly. She stepped over to the sink and washed her hands with the coldest water possible, calming even further. She didn't dare to look at herself in the mirror, because she knew what she'd find.

A woman on the brink of a complete collapse.

When Wyatt had first invited her to have Thanksgiving dinner with his family, Deirdre had resisted. She wasn't sure where that would put them in their relationship. But she'd had no idea that it would bring up all kinds of feelings about her own failures. How inferior she was as a daughter, a wife, a mother.

In fact, Deirdre wasn't any of those things, not here in Getaway Bay.

She was just a woman with a job. A wedding and party planner.

You're Wyatt's girlfriend, she told herself, finally looking up to meet her own eyes. At least her makeup hadn't smudged. She didn't look like she'd been crying, because she hadn't been.

"You can do this," she told herself. Even if she didn't want to. Even if she'd rather go home and eat a turkey sandwich and feed the stray cats on her street. She'd watch a Christmas movie, and miss her mom and her daughter, and everything would be normal.

But sharing her life with Wyatt and his family wasn't

inside her normal, and she didn't quite know how to do it. Didn't mean she *couldn't* do it.

And she liked Wyatt a lot, and she didn't want to embarrass him in front of his family. They were obviously important to him, and he spoke to them more than once a year. She didn't even do that.

Drawing in a deep breath, she opened the bathroom door and went back down the hall. Wyatt's brother had turned on a football game, and all of the men had abandoned the placemat craft at the table.

Deirdre stood in the mouth of the hallway and watched them. Scott and Wyatt high-fiving over something that had happened in the game. The women working in the kitchen, talking and cooking at the same time. Could she join them?

They seemed to have everything under control, and Deirdre didn't even know where she fit. Wyatt looked over his shoulder, obviously checking on her, and he jumped to his feet when he saw her hanging in the doorway.

He crossed the space toward her quickly and looked down into her face. "Hey. Are you okay?"

She nodded, because her voice was suddenly a ball in her throat, and she was choking.

"You don't have to make a placemat." He put his arm around her shoulders and shielded her from the eyes in the kitchen as he took her into the living room. "Come watch the game with us."

Deirdre sat on the couch, Wyatt beside her, his hand

anchored solidly in hers. This was okay. This was nice, even. Welcome and wanted. After several minutes, she relaxed further, her emotions evening enough for her to be able to talk.

More chips and dips were served, and Wyatt's sister came over and turned off the TV. "Enough, you guys. We're going on a family walk before dinner."

Surprisingly, no one argued, and Wyatt stood up and reached for Deirdre. They followed everyone else out the front door and Melinda turned toward the beach. Almost as if they were all being controlled by the same mind, they took their shoes off on the beach and left them in a pile, a couple of the teens running toward the water, leaving everyone else behind.

Deirdre realized that they knew what to do, because they'd spent many family occasions like this together. This wasn't their first walk on the beach. Or their first meal together. She was the only newcomer, and she found herself walking next to Amelia, also an addition to the family.

"Overwhelmed yet?" she asked.

"A little," Deirdre admitted. "I don't have any family down on this part of the island."

"I'm an only child," she said. "The first time I came to a family function with Scott, I was like, 'What in the world is this? How do I fit here?' I recognize that look in your eye." She smiled at Deirdre, and it meant so much to her.

"Any advice?"

"Let's see…agree with Laura nine times out of ten. And kiss Wyatt a lot."

"Oh, wow." Deirdre laughed, catching Wyatt's eye. "I wasn't expecting that."

"It's great to see him so happy again," Amelia said as one of her kids called for her. "He's been so lonely for so long." She gestured to her teenager. "Excuse me."

Deirdre watched her go, wondering what lonely looked like. She'd known Wyatt for a while now too, and she'd never categorized him as lonely.

"What did she say?" Wyatt asked, stepping around his brother to Deirdre's side.

"Nothing." She smiled up at him. "She's nice. I like her." She took Wyatt's hand in hers, almost desperate for the rest of the day to be as beautiful and tranquil as the beach was right now.

Dinner was a delicious and loud affair, but Deirdre survived. She didn't participate in the cornhole game after lunch but stayed inside to help with the desserts.

"And the crown jewel," Laura said, pulling a pie out of the oven. "Pumpkin pie."

"I don't like pumpkin pie," Deirdre said, and it felt like everything stopped. She glanced at Amelia and Melinda, but neither of them said anything.

"This is my grandmother's recipe," Laura said. "You'll like it."

But Deirdre wouldn't. Just looking at the dark orange baked custard made her stomach turn. But she whipped cream, added sugar to it, and helped with the egg whites for the lemon meringue pie. That one she would like, as Deirdre adored all things lemon.

"Pie," Melinda called out the back door, where the game of cornhole had devolved into touch football. The boys and men came back into the house, their voices so loud and the scent of sweat and earth coming with them.

Pies were cut and served, and literally everyone took a piece of the pumpkin pie. Deirdre didn't, because if they liked it, they should get to eat it. She didn't need to waste a piece on herself.

His mother saw her, and her lips pursed. She said nothing, though, and Deirdre felt like she'd dodged a bullet.

Wyatt's phone rang just as Deirdre had put her last bite of the delectable lemon meringue pie in her mouth.

"It's work," he said, rising from the table. His plate was clean, and he left it right where it was as he swiped on his call. "This is Chief Gardner."

"Ooh, Chief Gardner," Scott said, laughing at Wyatt as he retreated. The others at the table twittered too, and Laura shushed them.

"Leave him be," she said, cutting a look at Deirdre. "He's just doing his job."

"Come on, Mom," Scott said. "It was a joke."

"Wyatt's had a rough year," she said. "Now that he's back in counseling, he seems better." She pinned Deirdre with a look. "Don't you think, dear?"

"Oh, uh, we've only been seeing each other for a

couple of months." Deirdre cast a quick look at everyone at the table, and their gazes volleyed back to Laura.

"I'm quite surprised he brought you," she said.

Eyes back on Deirdre, who had no words.

"After his last break-up, he told me he wasn't going to date again." Eyes darted to Laura. "Apparently he's just not willing to be with someone who isn't Christine."

Everyone looked at Deirdre, and Amelia said, "Laura, I'm sure that's not true. He's only forty-four."

"Hey, sorry, everyone," Wyatt said, appearing at the table again. "I need to go." He looked at Deirdre. "Sorry, sweetheart. Duty calls."

Deirdre couldn't get up from the table fast enough, and she smiled her way out of the house, ready for sweatpants and some silence.

Chapter Seventeen

W yatt knew his mother had said something. What, he didn't know. But Deirdre had been white as a sheet when he'd turned back to the table. "Are you okay?" he asked, knowing he'd asked her a couple of times already.

"Your mother—something she said...."

Wyatt exhaled. "What was it? She just says stuff sometimes."

Deirdre's hands wound around and around each other, and Wyatt had never seen her do that before. "Hey," he said, reaching over and taking one of her hand in his. "What did she say?"

"She said you're not willing to be with anyone but Christine."

His heart shot to the back of his throat and then fell to his feet. "Well, that's just not true."

"It's not?"

"Deirdre," he said, not wanting to be angry at her. He was frustrated with the situation though. He didn't want to leave the family festivities early because of a house fire that had then yielded a marijuana stash once the fire department had arrived. Apparently, now there was weed-infused smoke drifting over an entire neighborhood in Getaway Bay. Who knew what would happen next?

And now his mother was saying stuff?

"Of course not," he said. "I told my mother that the day after Christine died. I don't feel that way anymore."

"She made it sound like you told her last week."

"Well, I didn't." He glanced at Deirdre. "Do you think I feel like that?" He'd kissed her with enough passion and need for her know that just wasn't true.

She shook her head and looked out the window.

"Then what's really going on? You've acted a little off today." He wasn't going to interrogate her, but he sure did want a relationship with a woman that was open and honest.

"I don't think I'm cut out for a family," she said.

"I don't want more kids," he said.

"It's more than that." She faced him, looking away again quickly. "That was really hard for me, Wyatt. Seeing the teenagers...so close to Emma's age. Having siblings and in-laws." She shook her head, her voice taking on a tortured edge. "That is just not my reality, and I don't fit. I'm just going to mess it up."

"Mess what up?"

"Them," she said, the word almost exploding out of her. "You. Your relationship with them." She sucked at the air, and Wyatt could see she was out of control now. Well, as out of control as Deirdre ever got. "I don't do families, Wyatt. I screwed up everything with my own mother, and you know how things are with my ex and my daughter." She pressed her lips together and shook her head, tight, angry bursts of movement.

"So we won't go to Christmas Eve dinner with them," he said as gently as he could. "It's no big deal."

"It's a big deal," she said. "Have you met your mother?"

"I can handle my mother."

"So you'll just go visit her yourself, and I'll be labeled the blonde woman who's stolen you away." She gave a bitter laugh. "Or worse." She shook her head.

Wyatt didn't know where this was going, but it wasn't a good place. "So…what? You don't want to be with me because I have a family who gets together for holidays?"

Deirdre said nothing, despite Wyatt giving her plenty of time and looking at her several times while he navigated the curves in the highway.

"Deirdre," he finally said.

"I think I need to take a step back, yes," she said.

Shock moved through Wyatt, and the only reason he kept breathing was because his lungs knew how to do it without any instructions from his brain. By the time he pulled into her driveway, the silence had accompanied them for half of the trip home.

"I'm sorry, Wyatt," she said. "Maybe you were right. Maybe I'm the one who's not ready for this."

He got out of the Jeep quickly, meeting her almost before she'd closed her door. "Deirdre, don't do this." He swallowed, so many things still left to say to her. "I really enjoy spending time with you. I want to be with you." He cleared his throat. "I'm falling in love with you. Please." He took her hand, and she looked down at their joined fingers.

"I need to think," she said, slipping her hand away from his. She slipped around him too, moving quickly up her steps and disappearing inside her house. Gone, like steam rising into the air.

Just gone. And Wyatt had the terrible, writhing feeling that he wouldn't be getting her back.

———

SEVERAL CITATIONS AND HOURS LATER, HE FINALLY pulled up to his house. Alone. He'd been hoping to bring Deirdre back here for coffee and cookies, as well as a Christmas movie. They'd talked about it and everything.

"Chief," his next-door neighbor, Prudence, called, and he sighed as he turned her way. The old woman carried a pie in her hands as she tried to cross the uneven lawn, and Wyatt jogged toward her.

"Pru," he said. "You're going to break another hip." He took the pie from her and steadied her with his free hand. Baked apples and cinnamon met his nose, and his mouth watered though he'd eaten enough to kill a small horse at lunch. Some of the guys who had to work today had brought in carved turkey and rolls, and he'd eaten at the station too. There was nothing better than a mashed potato slider with turkey and gravy and fresh bread, in his opinion.

"Oh, I'm fine," the woman said. "How was lunch as your mother's?"

"Good," he lied, though it was mostly true. "How was your daughter's cooking? Edible this time?"

"She catered, thank the heavens," Pru said. "Otherwise, I wouldn't have agreed to go."

"Do you want to come in for coffee?" he asked. "I bought cookies yesterday too, and Tigger would love to see you."

"Why do you think I brought out that pie?" She laughed in her raspy voice, and Wyatt smiled down at her. This wasn't exactly the date he'd been thinking of when he'd bought the red and white spiral cookies at the bakery yesterday. But he didn't really want to be alone either, and he and Pru had spent many evenings together since Christine's death. Before that, Pru was often in their home with Christine if Wyatt had something he had to do.

She'd sat with Christine on her last day on earth, even, and Wyatt loved the older woman as if she were his mother too.

"I think I may have lost Deirdre," he said once they were inside. He'd put Tigger out to take care of his business, and now he busied himself with making coffee.

Pru sat on the couch in the living room, and she called, "How? What happened?"

How could Wyatt explain without betraying Deirdre's confidence? "I don't know," he said. "I just don't think she's ready, especially to be part of a large family like mine."

Any family, she'd said. She'd told him that Dalton was unfaithful to her, and that was why they moved every few years and eventually she filed for divorce. He wasn't sure why that had taught her that a family wasn't worth having.

He knew she loved her daughter with the fierceness of gravity, and he could see her point about being around other teenagers being hurtful for her. So they wouldn't go around his mom's place until the teens were grown up. That wouldn't be that hard. Or he'd go alone.

But he could just see and hear how his mother would react to that.

Helplessness filled him, and he spooned sugar into a mug and poured a cup before the whole pot was finished. He took it to Pru and handed the mug to her. He sat on the coffee table in front of her.

"I really like her," he said. "But what if she's not ready?"

"Give her some time," Pru said. "She'll come around."

His phone bleeped out a warning noise, and Wyatt

got up to get it from the counter. He'd put it on silent after leaving his mother's house, but he had a setting where it would chime if the same number called three times within five minutes.

And the caller this time was his brother, Scott.

Annoyance flashed through him. He'd put his phone on silent for a reason, and Scott knew about Wyatt's emergency measures. The screen brightened again as he moved to the back door to let in Tigger, but Wyatt didn't answer his brother's call.

He had fifteen texts too, all of them in the family group message. Yeah, he wasn't going to read those right now either.

His mother had called; Melinda too. Eli, one of his officers who'd been on the scene at the pot fire today.

A weariness at being the Chief descended on him again, and he put the phone face-down on the counter and got down another mug. The only person he wanted to talk to was Deirdre, and she hadn't reached out once.

So tonight, he'd drink his coffee and eat his cookies, all while watching a cheery, romantic movie with Pru.

He'd decide what to do in the morning.

———

MORNING BROUGHT NO CLARITY, BUT WYATT DID TAKE Tigger to work with him. The day after Thanksgiving meant a ton of traffic in the downtown area, and nearly all the officers were out of the station that day. Norma always took the day off to go shopping with her daughters and her sister, and Wyatt enjoyed some alone-time in his office with the door closed.

He wondered what Deirdre did on days like today. He wondered if she'd had enough time to think. He wondered if he could stop by later and just check on her. Everyone wanted someone to check on them, didn't they?

Thinking about you this morning, he tapped out to her. *Are you okay?*

"Chief," someone said, opening his door before he could send the texts.

"Yeah, what?" He looked up to find the front desk officer standing there.

"There's a woman here. McKenna Lotus. She says her ex-boyfriend beat her up. Same guy who drove the car into the building a couple months ago."

Wyatt was up the moment Parker had mentioned McKenna Lotus. "Bring her in. I'll talk to her. Who else is here?"

"Just me and Georgia down in records."

"Get her to cover the desk. I need you with me," he said. "We want to make sure we're two deep on this."

He'd known Stephen Villalobos was bad, just like he knew Deirdre wasn't going to answer him even if he did text. His heart ached, and he wondered if he should text her, fight for her, or just let her go.

The very idea of not talking to her, not seeing her in

the evenings, not kissing her had his whole world in a tailspin.

But he followed Parker out to the front of the station to find McKenna Lotus crying, with a trickle of blood coming from her nose and her arm held delicately against her body.

Everything male and protective and angry inside him roared to life. "McKenna," he said. "Let's get you to the hospital."

"I didn't know where to go," she said, her voice too high. "And Bella has always said you're a friend."

Wyatt nodded to Parker, who jogged down the hall to the records room. "I just need to cover my front desk," he said. "And we'll go."

"He just came over, and—"

"McKenna," Wyatt said gently. "Let's wait until Parker's back. I want to do this by the book so this guy doesn't get off on a technicality." He sat next to her on the bench, but he didn't touch her. "Okay?"

She sniffled and nodded, and Wyatt took five seconds to look down at his phone.

He was going to fight for Deirdre, and he hit the *send* button.

Chapter Eighteen

D eirdre rolled over when she heard her phone buzz against the nightstand. She was awake anyway, and had been for about an hour. Just because she picked up her phone didn't mean she had to get out of bed.

Thinking about you this morning, Wyatt had sent. *Are you okay?*

Deirdre sighed as she looked up at the ceiling. The phone dropped to her chest, and she made no effort to pick it up again. Was she okay?

She honestly didn't know. What she did know was that spending the day with Wyatt's family yesterday had made everything clear in her mind. They simply existed on two different spheres right now, and his happy, loving family made everything about her family seem twice as bad.

And it was already bad.

Without thinking too hard about it, she picked up her phone. But she didn't text Wyatt.

Hey Dalton, she typed. *Would now be a good time to call?*

Because the protective order was between Emma and Deirdre, she could talk to Dalton. The judge had warned her to keep the communication as infrequent as possible, but he'd agreed that because they were Emma's parents, they needed to be able to talk.

Dalton could say no, of course. And he had full custody now. If he felt like Deirdre's questions or calls were inappropriate, he could file an injunction with the court. He never had, because Deirdre's calls and questions were never inappropriate.

Give me ten minutes, Dalton said. *I'm dropping Emma at surfing lessons, and then I'll be alone.*

Deirdre didn't respond. Ten minutes felt like forever, so she got up and got in the shower. That would make the time go faster, and she needed to do it anyway. She'd just stepped into a pair of joggers when her phone rang.

She lunged for it and swiped on the call from her ex-husband, her heart pounding beneath her breastbone. "Hello?"

"Deirdre," Dalton said, and he actually sounded happy to hear from her. "How are you?"

"Good," she lied. "Fine. You?"

Dalton chuckled, and it sounded like he was outside. Wind or waves came through the line, only drowned out when he said, "We're doing great."

Good. Fine. Great. Generic words for how people

were really doing. Dalton gave no details, and Deirdre hadn't expected any.

"Listen," she said. "I know it's a long shot, and you can just say no right now. But I'm wondering if Emma would consider withdrawing the protective order. I haven't been in town for almost twenty months now. I'm not going to contact her."

A healthy dose of silence came through the line. Finally, Dalton said, "Why, Deirdre? If you're not going to contact her—or come back to the North Shore—why does it matter?"

She wrapped her free arm around herself, trying to find an answer to the question. "I don't know," she finally said. "Just that it matters to me."

Dalton sighed as if she'd just asked him to give up both of his kidneys. "I can talk to her about it."

Tears filled Deirdre's eyes. "How is she?" she asked. "How was your Thanksgiving? What did you do?"

"She's doing great," he said, but his voice pitched up on the last word. "Thanksgiving was good. She made the turkey, and I did everything else. We ate with a few guys from down the beach who don't have family on the island. Spent some time on the beach."

Dalton was an expert at spending time on the beach. He worked at a beachside restaurant, and the man had been born with sand in his blood. "You love the beach," Deirdre said.

"What did you do?" he asked.

"Oh, uh, I went out to the Shark Fin Cove area."

"Huh. That's quite the drive. What's over there?"

Of course he would ask. Deirdre wasn't sure what to tell him. Would it be worse if she'd stayed home alone, or told him she had a boyfriend?

She wasn't sure why it mattered. Dalton had had many girlfriends besides Deirdre, most of them while he'd been married.

"My boyfriend's family lives over there," she said. "Well, his mother does. We ate at her place, only half a block from the beach."

"My kind of place," Dalton said without missing a beat. "How long have you been seeing this boyfriend?"

"A couple of months," Deirdre said. And she realized in that moment why everything had spiraled out of control yesterday. She wanted to share Wyatt with Emma. She wanted Emma to meet his siblings and have those other teenagers as step-cousins. She hated how isolated she'd become, and she hated that she couldn't have her family in her life the way others did.

"He's a nice guy?"

Deirdre sighed. "Dalton, you're not my father."

"No, I know. You're right." He exhaled. "Look, Emma is pretty much exactly like every other fifteen-year-old: self-centered. I don't know that I can convince her to drop the order. But I'll try. I've told her how asinine it is."

"You have?" Surprise filled Deirdre's heart. She'd never heard Dalton say that before. In fact, from her perspective, all Dalton had done was cheat on her, make life more difficult for her, and then take Emma's side with every lie that came out of her daughter's mouth.

But she couldn't turn her back on the girl. She was her daughter, and that meant something to Deirdre.

"Yes," Dalton said. "I'll talk to her but give me a few days. I have to bring things up…delicately."

Boy, did Deirdre understand that. "Okay," she said. "No rush. I appreciate you even saying you'll try." She drew in a deep breath. "Things are really okay?" She wasn't sure why, but her stomach was still knotted, and something just felt off.

"I'm getting another call. I'll call you back." The line went dead, and Deirdre let her hand holding the phone drop to her side. There was definitely something wrong, and Dalton just didn't want to say what it was. Deirdre knew, because she'd been on the receiving end of abruptly-ended phone calls exactly like that one before. And there'd been something wrong then too.

Dalton did not call back, not that Deirdre expected him to. She put out food for the strays, and then she pulled on her hiking boots and filled up her water sack for her backpack. She felt out of sorts too, but surely a hike through the rainforest would cure what was crooked in her mind.

By the time she returned to her backyard, the only thing happening was a violent cramp in her calf. Deirdre panted as she limped across the thin grass and up the steps to the back door. She was home. She'd done it.

She paused on the top step and stretched her calf,

groaning with the pain that felt so good. With the cramp finally subsiding, she went inside and filled up a glass with ice and water. She'd taken plenty to drink on the hike, but she'd been gone for six hours, and she needed more.

Her stomach growled, and she needed painkillers, so she set about getting a pan on the stove to make a grilled cheese sandwich. With that going, she downed a few pills and drank all the water.

Properly cheesed up, with toasty bread and lots of butter, Deirdre finally sat down at her dining room table. The silence in her house permeated everything, and she paused after eating half her sandwich to look around.

She wondered if Wyatt was working today. He kept a different schedule than most, as crime didn't take vacation days. Looking at her phone, she toyed with the idea of texting him back.

In the end, she didn't want to complicate her day. The hike through the lush trees, the air scented with hibiscus, had not helped with much—besides producing a couple of blisters and that calf cramp.

She finished eating, checked all the doors and windows to make sure they were locked, and grabbed her phone and a bag of lemon drops before heading for the bathroom. Dalton still had not called back, and at this point, Deirdre didn't think she'd hear from him for a while.

"If ever," she said, locking her bedroom door behind her. When she finally sank into the eucalyptus scented bath water, the steam rising into the air, Deirdre had found the calmest part of herself.

And it still vibrated with a quiet wail over walking away from Wyatt.

———

DEIRDRE WENT TO WORK ON MONDAY, PLENTY TO KEEP her occupied. She barely took a break for lunch, as Michelle DeGraw had thought she'd known exactly what she wanted for her wedding. But when Deirdre produced the three dress sketches, none of them were right. So Deirdre called in Ash Lawson, and they started from scratch. That meant more meetings. More talks about what Michelle really wanted. And a very awkward session where she'd actually brought another dress designer's drawings to Your Tidal Forever.

Deirdre knew it took all types to make the world go round, and she was getting paid to sit with Michelle and go over beads and lace. So she did.

She'd been meeting with her other bride too, who was only doing the reception through Your Tidal Forever, working with vendors to procure the items each bride wanted, and putting things in place for reception halls and venues for the I-do's.

In addition to that, she had the police department holiday party coming up. Most of the items for that had been decided upon and finalized, but she always met with clients with only a week to go before their big event.

But she put off calling Norma on Monday. And Tuesday. Before she knew it, it was Friday, and the department party was only seven days away. Finally, with only an hour left in the work week, she picked up the phone and called Norma.

"Norma Halstrom," she said. "What can I do for you?"

"Hi, Norma," she said. "It's Deirdre. I just need maybe twenty minutes with you on Monday or Tuesday to make sure we're on track for the party next Friday?" Why she'd ended it as a question, she wasn't sure.

"Oh, hello, Deirdre," she said loudly. "Monday or Tuesday, let me see what we have going on…."

Deirdre waited, her heartbeat speeding with every second that went by.

Norma finally said, "Monday at ten-forty would work," she said. "If you really only need twenty minutes. I have another meeting at eleven."

"I don't want to rush you," Deirdre said. Maybe she could get out of this. She'd have to see Wyatt at the party, probably, but it would be crowded with the whole department there. She could avoid him easily. Get in, get the food set up and the décor out, and disappear. She didn't work for the police department, and she didn't need to stay to mingle.

"Our schedule next week is insane," she said. "It's fine. This is how things are."

"Ten-forty then," Deirdre said. "I really will be quick."

"Sounds good, dear. See you then." Norma hung up, and Deirdre did too. Her heart felt like someone had raked it up and down on a washboard, wrung it out, and hung it up to dry. But in Hawaii, the humidity kept everything from truly drying, and now her most vital organ was starting to mold.

She hadn't texted Wyatt, and he'd only messaged one other time to let her know that they'd had a break in the vehicle-meets-building case. She'd wanted to celebrate with him, but honestly, it was easier to eat ice cream and barricade herself behind locked doors.

Sighing, she didn't notice right away when Meg entered her office. "What was that?" her best friend demanded.

"What?" Deirdre started organizing papers that were already neat.

"You broke up with the Chief?"

Deirdre gave a long, over-exaggerated sigh this time. "Yes, all right? And it took you a week to find out."

"Oh, I knew," Meg said, collapsing into the chair where Deirdre's clients usually sat. She picked up a mint from the bowl Deirdre kept on the front of her desk. "I was just waiting for you to say something."

"Nothing to say," Deirdre said.

"It wasn't over Emma, was it?"

Deirdre gave up trying to work. She tucked her hair behind her ear and leaned back in her chair. Meg was a good friend. She'd started at nearly the same time as Deirdre, and they'd worked together a lot to figure out the ropes at Your Tidal Forever. She had hair that sat between brown and auburn, and she was much more adventurous in the men she dated than Deirdre.

"I don't know," Deirdre said.

"How can you not know?"

"It was really because of his family," Deirdre said slowly, trying to figure out how to articulate how she felt. She hadn't been able to, which was why she'd never messaged Wyatt back.

"His family? They're that bad?"

"No," Deirdre said. "They're that good."

Sudden understanding entered Meg's expression, and Deirdre didn't need to say more. "Honey," she said. "You can't compare."

"Actually, I can," she said. "And it was almost insuf-ferable being with them. I'm not like them at all, and there's no way I'd ever fit." She got up and headed for the cupboard behind the door, where she stored her purse. "They reminded me of just how badly I want a family like theirs. And how royally I've screwed up. I don't need that in my life every time someone has a birthday."

She headed for the door, and Meg scrambled to her feet. "You're leaving?"

"Yes," she said. "I get here before everyone else every single day. I can leave thirty minutes early."

"Wait, what are you doing this weekend?" Meg all but ran in front of her, her eyes a bit wild now.

"Why? What's going on?"

Meg's vulnerability wasn't hard to see, and Deirdre couldn't believe she'd missed it. Just another failure to add to her list. She'd been so caught up in her own turmoil, she hadn't even seen Meg's.

"Why don't you and Father John come over for dinner tonight?" Deirdre suggested. "I'll make sushi, and we can swap Thanksgiving horror stories."

Meg's whole face lit up, and she said, "I'll be there at six."

Chapter Nineteen

Wyatt growled at anything and anyone that moved the week after Thanksgiving. He couldn't help it. Even helping McKenna Lotus file a protective order against her boyfriend and getting a hearing date set for that, as well as pursuing criminal charges for the man driving his car into the building where McKenna worked, had not lifted his mood as much as he'd hoped.

Deirdre had gone completely silent. Wyatt had originally thought he'd fight for her. Text her until she answered him. Stop by her place just to check on her.

But as he reviewed McKenna's order with her, he realized such things—unwanted contact. Repeated texts. Showing up at her house—could be considered stalking. Not that he believed Deirdre would ever file a protective order against him.

But he didn't want to pressure her to talk to him if

she didn't want to. The problem was, Wyatt had started to fall in love with her, and he missed her as much as he'd missed Christine when she'd died.

He was simply not fit to live alone, and by the time he got home on Friday night, he only wanted to leave again.

He'd been standing at Norma's desk when Deirdre had called, and he knew she'd be coming to the station on Monday morning. He just wasn't sure what he was going to do about it.

Tigger barked, and Wyatt said, "Yeah, bud. I'm coming." He opened the back door for the dog, who raced outside, his claws clicking against the deck. Wyatt stood at the door and looked up into the sky. Even December in Getaway Bay was beautiful, though the temperatures had cooled a little bit and there was talk of a gale hitting the island in ten days or so. The weathermen didn't like to talk too much about the weather until a few days out, as things changed in the ocean pretty quickly.

Wyatt didn't want to be home by himself. As Tigger took care of his business, he filled the dog's bowl and got down a leash from a cupboard in the kitchen. Tigger came back in, and Wyatt said, "Eat up, boy. We're going to go to the beach."

He'd find an empty room in some hotel and stay there for the night. *Can't do that with Tigger*, he told himself as the dog trotted over to his food bowl. He'd wanted to run away after Christine's death too, and he sort of had. He'd taken a long vacation, returning to the station three weeks later to dozens of flower arrangements, cards, notes, and words of encouragement.

Christine would've kept them all, so Wyatt had too. It had meant a lot to him that so many people had loved his wife, and he used to pull the cards and notes out to read them whenever he had a day where he missed Christine so much he could barely breathe.

But this break-up with Deirdre just had Norma shooting anxious glances toward his office and everyone in the department talking behind his back. He hated the sense of tension in the air at work, and he knew he was the cause of it.

He changed his clothes while Tigger ate, and then they left the house together. Wyatt's stomach complained for dinner, and he took the dog through the neighborhood as he considered taking the next week off.

Yes, December was a busy time. Lots of calls for shoplifting, and he usually needed three extra pairs of cops just for traffic control, both vehicular and pedestrian, around the shopping centers.

Wyatt walked on the path the led out of the neighborhood where he lived and into a more commercial part of the island. Certainly not downtown, but a few businesses lingered along this road, and tonight, in the sprawling park that backed up against his neighborhood, several food trucks had gathered.

The police officer in him had him scanning the crowd for danger, for anyone suspicious, for quick exits.

Determining he was safe, he turned his attention to his evening meal choices.

He decided on spam rolls and vegetable tempura from one truck, and Nutella cheesecake bites from another, taking his food and his dog to a picnic table out of the way. No one else sat there, but Wyatt could feel people looking at him. He was used to it, but tonight, he felt judged.

Tigger lay obediently at his feet, and he rewarded the dog with bits of spam and a couple of tempura carrots. He ate quickly and stood up, ready to be out of the spotlight. Why he'd thought coming out in public was a good idea, he wasn't sure.

"Let's go, boy," he said, leading the dog away from the crowd.

"Chief?" someone said, and he automatically turned toward them.

"Yes?" He appraised the young woman there, marking her as probably fifteen or sixteen years old. "Are you okay?"

"Yes." She smiled and pointed toward the tables. "My mom saw you eating alone and suggested you come eat with us."

He followed her finger to where a middle-aged woman sat at a table by herself. Horror struck Wyatt right behind the lungs. "Oh," he said, almost wishing for a robbery to take place right there in the park or for a natural disaster to hit the island.

No matter what, he couldn't go sit with that woman and her daughter.

He could get his own dates, and he hadn't come to the park to do that anyway.

"I'm finished now," he said, smiling at her in what he hoped was the kindest way possible. "I need to get home and check on my neighbor." Not entirely a lie, and Wyatt could easily swing by Pru's to see how she was doing. In fact, he would.

"Oh, okay," the girl said. "If you want her number, I'll give it to you." She wore the brightest look of hope on her face, and Wyatt didn't know how to say no.

"Oh, uh—" He cut off when his phone rang. "Excuse me." He didn't even look at the screen. He turned away from the teen and answered the call with, "This is Chief Gardner."

"Hey, man," Scott said. "Listen, I need some help with my lawn mower, and—"

"Yes," Wyatt said in a clipped tone. "It's fine, I can come. Yeah, don't even worry about it. These things happen." He looked at the teen and waved to her as he walked away. "I'll be right down."

"What is going on?" Scott asked.

Wyatt didn't dare answer until he'd put more distance between him and the teenager who'd tried to set him up with her mother.

"Are you using me to get out of something?" Scott asked.

"Yep," Wyatt said.

His brother laughed, adding, "I can't wait to hear about this. And I really do need help with my lawn mower."

Wyatt thought he was safe to speak now. "Okay, but I have to get home first. I'm out walking Tigger."

"Bring that new wrench set I got you for your birthday."

Wyatt laughed, realizing too late that this couldn't possibly be a tragic work emergency if he was chortling up a storm. Thankfully, a quick glance over his shoulder showed that the girl had gone back to her mother, and he was at least fifty yards away from them.

"Wrench set," he confirmed. "Got it."

"And I can't wait to hear what Deirdre had to say about the family," Scott said.

"I'm not talking about Deirdre," Wyatt said, leaving the park.

"Uh oh," Scott said. "Why not?"

"I'm just not. So I'll help you with your lawn mower, but I'm not discussing anything to do with my life, my job, or her."

That was that, and Scott knew it. He didn't even try to push Wyatt, for which he was grateful. They agreed to see each other soon, and Wyatt continued toward his house. Pru sat in her rocking chair on her front porch, and he called, "Want to go for a ride?"

She got up as quickly as an eighty-five-year-old woman with two hip surgeries in her past could. "Boy, do I ever."

Wyatt managed to smile as Tigger got in the back of the Jeep and he went to help Pru so she wouldn't be going in for surgery number three. He got her settled in the passenger seat, and ran inside to grab his keys.

If he'd have known she'd ask, "Whatever happened with Deirdre?" the moment he got behind the wheel, he wouldn't have invited her.

He looked at the older woman and saw his mother in her pale blue eyes. She hadn't asked him anything about Deirdre since Thanksgiving, and he wouldn't have told her the truth anyway.

But with Pru, he could. "You know what? She broke up with me, and I'm pretty devastated about it."

"Oh, my," Pru said. She looked sorry for only a moment, and then she shook the emotion away. "You know, I made tea three mornings ago, and I read the leaves for you. She was in them."

Wyatt smiled. He should've known Pru would bring up something psychic about how he and Deirdre were meant for each other. Heck, Deirdre had only come to his house maybe once or twice over the couple of months they'd been dating, and he'd never introduced her to Pru. But Pru had known about her anyway.

"She'll come back," Pru said, her voice strong. "The tea leaves never lie."

"They don't?" Wyatt shouldn't encourage her, but maybe if he kept her talking, he wouldn't have to.

"Nope," she said. "You know Terrance had to come crawling back to me, right? And he did. And boy, I made that man apologize." She chuckled, her voice catching in her throat. "Oh, how I loved him."

Wyatt could hear it in her voice, and he looked out the window on his side of the Jeep, watching the trees go past as he drove toward his brother's house.

"I think I'm in love with Deirdre," Wyatt said, almost to himself.

"She'll definitely come back," Pru said. "Love has a way of calling to a person, carefully inviting them to be in that circle where they're loved."

"Does it?" Wyatt asked, and this time, he truly wanted to know. Maybe he was a fool to hope Pru could be right. But he'd loved Christine with everything in him, and there was absolutely no way for love to call her back to him.

Pru continued to talk, always telling a story about her late husband. Wyatt thought he'd heard them all, but he apparently hadn't as she talked about a time when Terrance had worked on the coffee plantations on the island. He hadn't known that, and he was glad for the company as he drove.

When he pulled into his brother's driveway, he got a welcoming committee, and he cursed himself for saying anything about Deirdre.

"Just real quick," Amelia said. "Did she like the family or not like us?"

"It's got nothing to do with that," Wyatt said.

"I just liked her so much." Amelia actually looked

worried. "And you two seemed just perfect for each other."

"Amy," Scott said. "I said he didn't want to talk about it."

"And what? We're just going to let him slip back into his shell? That's no way for him to live." She looked at Wyatt, her eyes blazing now. He'd always gotten along with his brother's wife, and in fact, Amelia had been the biggest comfort in the days and weeks following Christine's death, as Wyatt tried to figure out how to console Jenn and himself.

"Sorry, but it's not," she said. "You were different at Thanksgiving, Wyatt. *So* happy. And I know it was because of her."

"So what if it was?" he asked.

"She'll come back," Pru said.

"Drop this, Amy," Scott warned.

The four of them looked around at each other, all eyes finally coming back to Wyatt. He was so tired of people looking at him, trying to size him up, yearning to figure out how he felt.

"Maybe call her," Amelia suggested.

"I texted."

"But maybe you should call," she insisted, to which Pru added, "Calling is always better than texting."

"I'll take the wrench set." Scott relieved Wyatt of the wrenches and turned toward the open garage.

Wyatt held up both hands to the two women still in front of him. "Ladies, believe it or not, I can handle my love life." With that, he walked away from them, pure humiliation flowing through him.

Not only that, but now he was a liar too, because he had no idea what he was doing. He wanted to get back together with Deirdre, but he wasn't going to call her. She knew his number too, and she was the one who'd said she needed to take a step back.

Chapter Twenty

Deirdre entered the police station on Monday morning before ten-thirty, and she knew instantly that Wyatt wasn't in the building. How she knew, she didn't know. But she knew.

Her muscles relaxed, and she hadn't even realized how tense she'd been. Her fingers unclenched as she went through the metal detector after laying her files on the security belt. The hustle and bustle of the place should've calmed her, but all it did was heighten her awareness.

Norma sat at her desk, and Wyatt's door was closed, the office beyond it dark. His secretary caught her looking, and she said, "He's not in today. He took the whole week off."

Deirdre swung her attention back to Norma. "He did? Will he be at the party?"

"I told him if he wasn't, I'd skin him alive," Norma

said, and Deirdre believed her. She wouldn't want to be on this woman's bad side. She may look like the sweet grandmotherly type, what with her graying hair and wrinkles around her eyes, but she was still sharp as a tack and not to be trifled with.

"Okay," Deirdre said, sitting in front of her desk. "I promised to be fast. I just want to go over everything one final time and update you as to where we are." She opened the folder and saw the order for the food. "Every-thing is set for the chicken sandwiches and the crab cakes," she said. "I talked to Claudia at Mussel's, and she confirmed a four-thirty set up time."

She paused so Norma could ask a question or make a comment, but she just nodded.

"We'll have the profiteroles, as well as an array of drinks," she said. "Hot and cold. Nuts About Dough has confirmed the setup of the doughnut wall at three-thirty. I guess it takes about an hour. I'll be here by two to get the place decorated, and I believe you said you wanted a real tree. Tell me more about that."

"Well, just look at that thing." Norma gestured to the sad-looking Christmas tree near the door. "Half of the lights are burnt out."

"So you don't necessarily mean a real pine tree. A living one. You just want it to be more festive."

"Yes," she said.

"Well, I think it'll be festive," Deirdre said, turning a page. "I got the final mockups for the décor from Bruce this morning, and this is what he'll be doing." She showed Norma the full-color printout, which included where the food would be, the additional Christmas tree, a sack of gifts that Norma herself would be providing, and a station to get setup to receive texts from Santa.

"It's beautiful," Norma said, and she sounded choked up. Sure enough, when Deirdre looked at her, she was dabbing at her eyes with a tissue. "I have some allergies," she said.

Deirdre didn't believe her for a second. No one had allergies in December, when there was very little pollen in the air.

"I believe we're doing some brief caroling," she said. "I have all the tracks on a thumb drive. You said I could use a computer hooked to some speakers here?"

"That's right," Norma said, fully composed now. "We'll man the music from my station right here."

"Perfect. And then gifts. Done." Deirdre closed the folder. "That's for you. If there's anything you need between now and Friday, let me know."

"I'll make sure the desks are moved," Norma said, and Deirdre nodded as she stood. She loved short meetings, and she loved keeping her word to keep them short. She couldn't help looking toward Wyatt's door one more time, and Norma caught her.

"You know, he'd take you back in a heartbeat."

Deirdre's every defense went up. She did not want to talk about her personal life with anyone, least of all her boyfriend's secretary.

Ex-boyfriend.

She sighed. "Thank you, Norma. See you Friday." She walked out of the police station with her head held high, remembering the last time she'd had to make a conscious effort to do that. Wyatt had come running after her then.

He didn't this time.

She stewed over what to do about him as she drove back to work. She'd spent most of the weekend with Meg and her dog, Father John. They'd gone paddle boarding and spent hours on the beach, reading, drinking fruity slushes, and talking. Mostly about Meg and what kind of man she wanted, but Deirdre had opened up a little bit. And by that, she meant she hadn't shut completely down when Meg had asked about Wyatt.

But the answer was always the same.

I don't know.

———

A FEW DAYS LATER, DEIRDRE SAT ON HER COUCH, THE plan for the department party spread all over the coffee table in front of her. Setting up for a party of this magnitude was no small matter, and she had two pages of notes, with what needed to be done in what order to maximize the time she had.

Sometimes she took an assistant with her to setup and monitor the party, but Christmas was one of the busiest seasons for weddings, parties, and celebrations. While the actual holiday was still two weeks away, everyone wanted to get their party or show done so they could enjoy the holidays with their families.

Her phone rang, and she glanced at it. "Dalton." She nearly fell forward in her haste to grab the phone, and she couldn't keep the anticipated hush out of her voice when she answered with, "Dalton?"

"Hello, Deirdre," he said, immediately clearing his throat. That wasn't good. Or maybe it was. She'd heard him do it so many times over the years, usually right before he came clean about something.

"What's going on?" She forced herself to only ask the one question, though many more piled behind her tongue.

"Your daughter wants to know what you're doing this weekend."

Someone else spoke on his end of the line, and Deirdre's whole heart trembled. Had that been Emma?

"Tomorrow," he clarified. "Emma would like to know what you're doing tomorrow afternoon and evening."

Deirdre's mind blanked. Whatever she had on her schedule, she'd clear. She looked down, everything spinning wildly out of control.

She saw the papers on the coffee table. The party. "I have a huge event," she said. "The holiday party for the police department here in Getaway Bay." She thought quickly, not wanting to lose this opportunity. "But I'm free Saturday and Sunday. I could come up there."

Scuffling and low-level talking came through the line. Deirdre hated this feeling of helplessness, mingled with desperation. Would she get in trouble for seeing Emma, if her daughter initiated it? She wasn't sure how all the rules of the protective order worked, and she should probably call her lawyer the moment she got off the phone with Dalton.

"Apparently, Emma has some play practices," Dalton said. "But she has agreed to perhaps get together with you. Have dinner or coffee."

Deirdre just kept breathing, the movement in her lungs coming faster and faster with every moment. "That's great," she managed to say.

"We're going to the courthouse in the morning to find out about dismissing the protective order. I'll let you know what we discover."

"Thank you, Dalton," Deirdre said, on the verge of tears. She didn't want him to hear that though, and she straightened and took a deep breath.

"Can you hold on a sec?" he asked.

"Yes." Deirdre waited, listening intently though he'd obviously tried to hold the phone away from his mouth. He told Emma to leave, that he wanted to say something to Deirdre without being overheard.

Her heart continued to pound, faster and faster still.

"Are you still there?" he finally asked.

"Yes," she said.

"Look, she's upset with me because I want to tell you everything."

"Okay." Deirdre wasn't sure what he wanted her to say. "I've never asked for that. Only what you or she wanted to give me." Which had been almost nothing since she'd left the North Shore. The longest she'd gone without hearing from Emma or Dalton was seven months. Seven long, painful months where she had no idea if her family was even alive. And the only reason she'd texted then was because the island had been hit with a tsunami, and she'd finally had a reason to text to ask them how they were.

Still alive, had been his response.

"She's not doing well," he said. "And I don't know how to get her to do anything. She's flunking out of school, hanging out with the wrong kids. I've even caught her vaping a couple of times." He sighed, and he sounded so frustrated. Deirdre held the phone to her ear, numbness spreading through her.

She didn't know what to say, though the vindictive part of her wanted to throw everything he'd ever said to her about how overbearing and controlling she was right back in his face. He'd had no idea what it was like to raise Emma alone—and that had started long before the actual divorce.

She supposed he did now, and that was probably punishment enough. "I'm so sorry, Dalton. She's not an easy kid."

"No, she is not."

Deirdre thought, her mind moving through different solutions. But the truth was, she didn't live on the North Shore anymore, and she wasn't going back. "So, what are you going to do?"

199

"I proposed that we think about moving down to Getaway Bay," he said. "We could co-parent easier there, and she could ease into having you in her life again."

Deirdre blinked rapidly, turning around as if someone would be there to tell her this was all a dream. "Is that what she wants?"

"She doesn't know what she wants," Dalton said with another sigh. "And she doesn't get to make all the decisions."

"I won't see her or talk to her until the protective order is out of play," Deirdre said. "I have to protect myself, and if I say something wrong about her hair, I don't want her crying wolf again." Her own vitriol, though slight, surprised her. She'd spent so many months pining for a relationship with her daughter, and yet not just any relationship.

A healthy one.

"We'll find out about that tomorrow, and I'll let you know."

"Thank you for telling me how things really are." And they weren't good, fine, or great. "Is she going to be able to graduate?" Students had to take a certain number of classes—and pass them. Just because Emma was only fifteen didn't mean her grades didn't count for anything.

"She has to retake a math class," he said. "And maybe this English class she's currently failing if she can't get the grade up by the middle of January."

"Okay," she said, because what else was there? She couldn't give Dalton parenting advice.

He cleared his throat. "And Deirdre? I just wanted to say I'm sorry too. For everything. For believing her over you. For not getting her to dismiss this silly protective order before it even went before the commissioner. For all of it."

Deirdre's throat closed. This was what families did. They talked. They forgave. They came together to heal.

She didn't say it was okay, because it wasn't. "Thank you," she said again. "Let me know what you learn at the courthouse tomorrow." She could research it online too, but she fell back to the couch after the call had ended.

Hope shone in her soul for maybe the first time in eighteen months. She'd experienced some level of joy and happiness since arriving in Getaway Bay. But she'd never really felt hopeful.

She warmed, and her excitement grew. She jumped up, grabbing her phone, and she called the one person she wanted to share this news with. Share her life with.

Wyatt.

"Deirdre?" he answered. "What's going on? Are you okay? Where are you?"

Tears sprang to her eyes at the simple sound of his beautiful, deep voice. She couldn't speak over the lump of emotion in her throat.

"Deirdre," he said. "Can you speak, sweetheart? What's wrong? Is someone in the house?"

"No," she managed to say. "Can you come over?"

Only one breath passed before he said, "I'm on my way."

And in that moment, Deirdre knew she didn't deserve a man as good, as loyal, as kind as Wyatt Gardner. But she wanted him all the same.

For the first time since they'd started dating, she had hope. Hope for a better future with her daughter. Hope for a life she wanted to live. And hope that she could learn to trust and love a man again.

If she'd have known she needed hope to light her way, she'd have started searching for it earlier.

"It doesn't matter," she said, tears spilling down her cheeks. She had it now, and that was all that mattered. And *hope*fully, she'd be able to set things right with Wyatt too and get him back into this new, hopeful life she wanted to lead.

Chapter Twenty-One

W yatt drove on the erratic side from his house to Deirdre's, which was only about ten minutes. She'd claimed she was okay, but she'd barely been able to speak. He couldn't help the paths his imagination took, and he envisioned everything from her being gone from the house to chilling on the front steps with his favorite pizza.

His heart bobbed around inside his chest, nothing anchoring it. He thought of her stories about how she'd come to love lemon drops, and he really hoped the call had stemmed from something good, not something sinister.

He turned onto her lane and approached her house a little slower than he'd been driving. Nothing seemed out of the ordinary. Her car sat in the shallow driveway, and the door was closed. After pulling next to her, he jumped from his Jeep and hurried to the front door, calling, "Deirdre?"

"Just a sec," she said, and that was good. She could speak now.

Wyatt remained on high alert, scanning left and right as if the danger would present itself from there.

She opened the door, and Wyatt knew the most dangerous thing was now standing in front of him.

He found himself unable to speak as he took in her yoga pants. The tight pink T-shirt with the words Team Bride across the chest. She wore bare feet and her hair piled up on her head in a messy bun.

"Hey," she said, and while her voice was strong, a river of uncertainty flowed through her eyes. He felt the same thing cascading through his whole body. Her chin trembled, and Wyatt took her into his arms.

She cried against his chest, and Wyatt let his own emotions storm through him too. "It's okay," he said several moments later. "Let's go inside." He wasn't sure what kind of neighbors Deirdre had, as she kept so many people at arm's length. She hadn't spoken of them much, and Wyatt hadn't even seen that warning sign that she might not be ready for a relationship with him.

He'd always thought it was him who needed to overcome certain hurdles.

They went inside, and Deirdre kept her face turned away from him while she wiped her eyes. "I'm sorry," she said. "Something happened, and I wanted to tell someone." She lifted her eyes to his then. "I wanted to tell *you.*"

Wyatt's chest vibrated with every breath, but he didn't know what to say.

"Wyatt, can we try again?" She folded her arms and looked at him with a level of vulnerability that made him want to erase every bad thing from her life. "I made a mistake," she said. "About us. You are the one of the best things in my life, and I don't know why I didn't...." She shook her head. "I need all the good things I can get."

He studied her for a moment, already knowing he'd take her back over and over again. "I know you internalize things differently than I do," he said. "But I'm willing to be by your side through whatever happens."

"You are?"

"Of course." He approached her and took her hands in his. "Deirdre, I'm falling in love with you, and I hope that doesn't scare you. We can go slow. I'm not in any hurry."

Deirdre closed her eyes and leaned her forehead against his chest. "I'm falling in love with you too."

Wyatt shut his eyes too and tipped his head back. Being loved was the best feeling in the world, and he couldn't believe he got to experience it twice.

"I called Dalton."

Wyatt snapped his eyes open. "Your ex-husband?"

Deirdre smiled as she stepped back. "Yes, and he's going to the courthouse tomorrow to find out how to cancel the protective order. That was why I called you. I wanted you to know."

"Wow." Wyatt didn't know what else to say. He honestly didn't care why she'd called, only that she had. It didn't matter that he'd just ordered dinner from FoodNow—his chest squeezed. "I have food coming to my house."

Deirdre started laughing, and Wyatt pulled out his phone. "Give me a second. I'll see if they can deliver it here. Then you're going to tell me the whole story." He tapped and found that the driver hadn't left the Hawaiian barbecue joint he'd ordered from.

He looked up as Deirdre quieted. "Thank you for coming," she said, everything laid out between them.

Wyatt abandoned the app and tossed his phone onto the couch. He took Deirdre's face in both of his hands and looked right into her eyes. "I'll always be here." He kissed her, and she kissed him back.

The past two weeks of misery melted off of his shoulders, and he couldn't believe this good woman had chosen him.

———

AN HOUR LATER, WYATT AND DEIRDRE HAD FINISHED ALL of the pulled pork and macaroni salad, and she'd told him everything about Dalton and Emma.

"So what are you going to do?" he asked. They currently sat on her couch, and Wyatt had her tucked against his side while he leaned back. He was full and warm and absolutely content to stay with Deirdre until she kicked him out.

"He's going to call in the morning," she said. "And if they really do file the paperwork to cancel the order, I'm going to wait until the judge says for sure that it's over."

"Of course," he said. "But then what?"

"I don't know," Deirdre said. "Honestly, I don't. She hasn't changed, and while I want to be able to text her and go to any store I want without fear of running into her and getting arrested, I'm not sure I need to open myself up to get hurt again."

Wyatt considered her. "I understand that," he said. "And it's smart. Maybe it'll just be a slow healing process." He gave her a small smile. "I've been through that."

She snuggled deeper into his side, and satisfaction and love moved through Wyatt. "I'm sorry I freaked out about your family."

"I've already forgotten about it," he said. "But you made an impression on Amelia and Scott. When I told them you'd broken up with me, Amelia was very worried."

"Oh yeah? Why's that?"

Wyatt pressed his lips to her forehead. "She seems to think you make me happy. That you're perfect. Oh, and Pru—my next-door neighbor—said you'd come back because she read it in her tea leaves one morning." He chuckled, glad when she joined in with him.

She tipped her head back, and Wyatt claimed her lips. "And to be clear," he whispered, barely putting any space between them. "You do make me happy. And I think you're perfect for me too."

She didn't have to speak to give him the best response in the world. She simply kissed him again.

———

"That tree skirt goes on the tallest tree," Deirdre said the next day. "Wyatt, can you move that last desk for me, please?"

He did what she said, because the stress level inside the police station was at an all-time high, and all they were doing is decorating for the holiday party.

But Deirdre had descended on the station with boxes and bins and her friend Meg, and Norma had not been ready. So Wyatt had jumped up from his desk and started moving things where Deirdre wanted them. As the minutes passed, the tables got set up and covered. The trees decorated. The gifts placed just-so on the tree skirts.

Meg lit candles that smelled like pine trees and snow, and while Wyatt had never seen snow or a pine tree, it felt exactly like a white Christmas. Not that he'd ever had one of those either.

Deirdre had though, and she beamed around at the normally industrial space and said, "Now this feels homey."

She'd pushed all the desks to the sides of the room to

create more space. The trees and food tables sat against the back wall, and long tables took up the newly opened space. They held the candles, as well as silverware in red and silver and green napkins.

Deirdre moved over to Norma's computer and started fiddling around with the music. Several minutes later, Meg called, "Food's here," and several people started carrying in the crispy chicken sandwiches Wyatt had loved.

"And crab cakes," he said as Deirdre arrived at the food table. Several other officers had already started to crowd nearby.

"Nobody is to touch a single thing," she said to them. "Until the party starts."

"Yes, ma'am," Wyatt said, because he didn't want to upset Deirdre. She'd worked very hard on this party, and he wanted it to be everything she'd planned.

She hovered over the punch, over the profiteroles, over the placement of every tray and every serving utensil. She double-checked the doughnuts hanging from pegs on the doughnut wall that had been tempting Wyatt for two solid hours.

She conferred with Meg and Norma, and precisely at five o'clock she nodded at Norma, who came over to Wyatt. "Call them to order, Chief," she said.

Wyatt stepped over to the nearest desk and picked up the phone there. He dialed the appropriate numbers to get the public address system to activate, and he waited for the beep.

"Ladies and gentlemen," he said. "This is Chief Wyatt Gardner, and we're ready to begin our police department party in the main room. Anyone with anything to do with the police department is welcome." He met Deirdre's eye, a slip of foolishness running through him. But she'd asked, and he'd agreed to say the next part. Her eyebrows raised as another moment passed.

"Ho ho ho!" he boomed into the receiver. "Merry Christmas." He hung up and grinned at her while laughter burst out of everyone already standing in the room. Everyone who came through the door was also smiling, and Wyatt could see the wisdom in Deirdre asking him to act like this party was exactly what he wanted.

Maybe it was, and maybe it wasn't.

But as he took her into his arms and kissed her, he knew that *she* was exactly what he wanted.

Even with everyone looking, catcalling, and clapping.

Chapter Twenty-Two

D eirdre and Wyatt spent Christmas at his place, with Pru from next door and his dog, Tigger. At least that was the plan.

A couple of days before Christmas, Deirdre found out Meg wasn't going to go home for the holidays, and she'd invited her and Father John to come to the meal. She'd no sooner stepped foot inside her office to tell Wyatt when her phone rang.

"Hey," she said. "I was just about to text you."

"Don't be mad," he said. "But I found out a friend didn't have anywhere to go for Christmas, and I invited them to our dinner."

"Oh—"

"And I may have invited Cal and his family too," he said. "You're friends with Lisa, right?"

Deirdre started laughing, and Wyatt did too. "I just invited Meg and her dog," she said. "Sounds like we better get to the grocery store again." They'd gone last night to buy everything, and Wyatt had it all at his house, just waiting to be prepared.

"I'm headed out right now to get more chocolate oranges. I'll get another dog treat too."

"Not everyone has to have gifts," Deirdre said.

"Yes, they do," Wyatt responded. "I'll get several extras, just in case."

"In case of what?" she asked. "Are you going to invite more people?"

"Who knows?" He laughed again. "I just don't think anyone should be alone on Christmas Day, and I have a big place. It won't kill me to store some chocolate oranges."

"Store them, right," Deirdre said sarcastically. "If there are any left, you'll have those consumed before New Year's."

He didn't deny it, and Deirdre liked that she knew such intimate details about him. The last couple of weeks since they'd gotten back together had been great, and while she didn't feel the need to accelerate their relationship either, she knew they were playing a long game. A marriage game. One where her uniform was a wedding dress.

She sat down at her desk and tapped to get her laptop awake. The wedding board she'd started when she'd first come to Getaway Bay and Your Tidal Forever was still there, staring back at her.

She'd started pinning things that she personally liked,

things she might want at her own wedding. Her wedding with Wyatt.

Her heart shot out an extra beat, but she wasn't afraid. She wasn't worried about what she might have to tell him. She was excited to share her life with him.

Dalton had called and said he and Emma had filed the cancellation paperwork, but the hearing wasn't until after the New Year. So she'd endure one more Christmas alone, though she couldn't help wondering how much she'd want Emma in her life. She'd been communicating with Dalton a lot more, and it certainly seemed like their daughter had not changed a whole lot.

Deirdre had been telling herself that for a couple of weeks now. Everything was not going to go back to normal. A new normal would have to be established. She couldn't control Emma, and she didn't have to open herself up for more pain and more damage to have her daughter in her life.

"When are you done today?" he asked.

"Four," she said. "And then a whole week off." She sighed just thinking about having a little vacation. She wasn't leaving the island, but she was planning to visit a different beach every day once Christmas passed. She and Meg were planning that, actually, and Deirdre had been packed for a couple of days already. "Is your mother still okay for me and Meg to stay with her for a night?"

"Are you kidding?" Wyatt asked. "It's all she talks about. I get new texts from her everyday. What does

Deirdre like to eat? Do you think she'd tell me about her job? Maybe I can get her to stay an extra day." He pitched his voice up in a bad imitation of his mother.

Deirdre burst out laughing, and Wyatt chuckled with her. "You've made her whole year by asking to stay overnight."

"And you're still okay not coming?"

"Sweetheart," he said. "I was married for over twenty years. I understand that women need some time to themselves sometimes. You're coming off something stressful, and then going into the hearing. I have plenty to keep me busy until you get back."

"Okay," she said. "And then, maybe we should plan something off-island in the springtime."

"Off-island? Like a trip together?"

"Yes," Deirdre said, feeling reckless and a bit unlike herself. "I've never done that before, but I would like to meet your daughter."

"Oh, you're talking way off-island," he said, clearly surprised.

"Yes," she said. "I'll send you something."

"Okay," he said, and the call ended. Deirdre sat down in front of her computer again. She'd started piecing together things to do in California, and she sent Wyatt the link for the board where she'd been putting things.

Wow, he texted back. *I'm calling Jenn right now.*

Deirdre smiled, because his enthusiasm for what she wanted made her happy.

CHRISTMAS MORNING DAWNED SOMEWHAT RAINY. DEIRDRE drove over to Wyatt's and found him in the kitchen wearing a pair of gym shorts and a gray T-shirt. "Hey, sweetheart," he said, pausing in his washing of his dog's bowl to kiss her. "You're early."

"Couldn't sleep." She bent down and gave Tigger a good scrub behind his ears.

Wyatt put his food bowl down and said, "I'll go shower."

"I'm going to get the turkey in," she said, setting her purse on top of his fridge. She got to work, putting plenty of salt and pepper in the butter she then rubbed under and all over the turkey's skin.

She wasn't stuffing the bird, as they were having candied ham too. Plenty of mashed potatoes. A huge salad, along with fried plantains, shrimp cocktails for appetizers, and freshly baked rolls for days.

She'd barely slid the turkey into the oven when Wyatt returned. "Can I interrupt you for a minute?" he asked.

Deirdre stepped over to the kitchen sink to wash her hands. "Yeah, give me a sec to wash up." Fully soaped and drying her hands, she turned to find him wearing a pair of jeans and a dark brown sweater with Christmas lights sewn into the collar.

"What in the world?" she asked, giggling at his wardrobe. "I've never seen you wear anything like that."

He glanced down at his sweater, smiling.

"The collar lights up and everything." Deirdre stepped over to him and touched one of the little green lights. "How does it do that?"

"Christine made it for me," he said. "It has a little battery pack back here." He touched the back of his neck. "I wear it every Christmas."

Deirdre gazed up at him, so much love streaming through her. "You must miss her so much."

He swallowed. "Sometimes," he said. "Not today, though."

"No?"

"No." Wyatt leaned down and kissed her, and Deirdre didn't care that she had a long list of tasks in front of her. Wyatt was the best gift in her life, and she wanted him to know it.

He finally cleared his throat and stepped away from her. She leaned against the fridge now, and she had no idea how she'd gotten there. "I wanted to give you my gift before the others come," he said.

Moving over to the Christmas tree in his living room, Wyatt plucked something from the branches of the tree. Deirdre followed him, her heart pounding in the back of her throat.

"I know I said we could go slow," he said. "And we can. Pick any date you want, even years from now." Wyatt cracked the lid on a little black box to reveal a diamond ring. "I just want to be yours every Christmas."

Deirdre pulled in a breath and stared at the glittering gem. Then Wyatt.

"I love you, Deirdre," he said. "Will you marry me?"

She drew in a breath, her lungs shaking. Her fingers shaking. Her very soul shaking with excitement. "Yes," she whispered.

Wyatt grinned and swept her into his arms, lifting her right off the ground. Deirdre laughed with him, tears accompanying the giggles as he slid the ring on her finger. "I love you too, Wyatt," she said.

He swayed with her, and Deirdre enjoyed the moment where only the two of them existed, where she could listen to him breathe and know he was hers. She was his.

"I really am going to retire next fall too," he said. "I've decided."

Deirdre pulled away from him and searched his face. "And then what?"

"I don't know," he said. "But I'm going to call the university once classes start again in January. I could definitely do something for them. They've asked me before, and I like working with new recruits."

Deirdre beamed up at him. "I don't think we need to be engaged for very long."

"No?"

"I want Meg to do my wedding, so I'll check her schedule and pick the soonest date she has."

"You're sure?"

Deirdre grinned and nodded. "I'm sure."

Tigger barked, and they both turned toward him. "Someone's here," Wyatt said.

"Must be Meg," Deirdre said. "She's making her pumpkin roll here this morning."

Sure enough, the doorbell rang, which sent Tigger into a barking fest, and Wyatt opened the door to welcome Meg to his home.

Deirdre squealed and held out her left hand. "I want you to plan the wedding."

"The wedding?" Meg struggled under the weight of her grocery bags, and Wyatt relieved her of several of them. "Oh my holy dolphins and starfish," Meg said, her voice turning to air. She looked from Wyatt to Deidre. "You're engaged."

"We're engaged!" Deirdre shrieked.

"Ho ho ho!" Wyatt said, and the three of them laughed.

Meg hugged Deirdre and started swiping on her phone, talking a mile a minute about her schedule and the brides she already had to deal with. "Oh, and one more thing. We have room for one more, right? I invited Texas."

It was Deirdre's turn to be surprised. "You did?"

"Yeah, he didn't have anywhere to go, and I just found out." She glanced at Wyatt, who was loading his coffee mug into the dishwasher.

"Wyatt will have to give up one of his hoarded chocolate oranges," she teased.

He smiled at her and came to put his arm around her shoulders. "We have room. Who is it?"

"Her new boyfriend," Deirdre teased, but Meg shook her head.

"Not my boyfriend. You know him, Wyatt. I met him at the police department party. Dallas Farnsworth?"

"Oh, Dallas, sure," Wyatt said, but he looked confused. "I thought you said Texas."

"He goes by Texas," Meg said. "In his biker club thing."

"Oh."

"That's what I said," Deirdre said. "But Meg says he's a good guy."

"He works in the evidence room," Wyatt said. "I didn't know he was a biker club guy."

"He is," Meg said. "It's not like they're outlaws, Wyatt. He was explaining it to me, and it sounds like they do good things around the community. Bikers for Babies? That's their main cause."

"I have heard of that," Wyatt said. "And they do good things for babies born prematurely and babies born addicted to drugs and alcohol."

"Exactly." Meg moved into the kitchen. "I better get started. We have a pumpkin roll to make this morning and a wedding to plan!"

Nine months later

Wyatt tugged on the ends of his jacket sleeves, more nervous than he'd ever been. More than when he'd flown across the Pacific Ocean with Deirdre at his side so she could meet his daughter. More than when he'd met Emma for the first time. More than when he'd worked his last day as Chief, and more than when he'd walked into his beginning criminology class at the university the next Monday.

He was getting married today, and he had no right to be this nervous. He'd done this before, after all, and Deirdre was going to show up.

She'd wanted a beach wedding, and Wyatt hadn't objected. She'd wanted it in September, when they'd started dating again, and Wyatt was fine with that. She'd wanted it to be small and personal, and Wyatt had said he'd try.

Unfortunately, he'd been Chief of Police in Getaway

Bay for a very long time—and for their entire engagement. The news of his marriage to Deirdre had been on the local news and in the local newspaper for weeks now.

The whole town was coming. In fact, they were showing it on television.

"Ready, Boss?" someone asked, and he turned toward his brother.

"I can't find my cufflinks," he said, glancing down at the table in front of him. He and Deirdre had planned a family-only ring ceremony to take place before the wedding. That way, she got the private moment she wanted, and the people on the island who'd loved Wyatt got to participate too.

"Take mine," Scott said, already unbuttoning his links.

"I can't take yours," Wyatt said. "Jenn got these for me, specifically for the wedding." His daughter wasn't there, because she was pregnant and due any day now. Her doctor had not allowed her to fly for so long over open water for the wedding. Deirdre had said they could do it at another time, but Jenn wouldn't hear of it.

"They're literally right there," Scott said, picking them up from the corner of the table. "You're blind, man."

"I'm nervous," Wyatt said, looking at his brother before focusing on the cufflinks.

"Why?"

"I don't know. I've just had a lot of changes in my life recently."

"It's going to be great." Scott took over and got the cufflinks on. "You look great. We're waiting for you."

Wyatt looked at himself in the mirror and decided this was as good as it was going to get. "Okay. I'm ready too." He followed his brother out into the main room, where the small group Deirdre had wanted waited.

She stood there, and she rendered Wyatt mute. She wore a white gown that seemed glued to her upper body, with straps that went over her shoulders and left a lot bare. The skirt flared at the waist, and flowed to the floor, covered with lace and beads and everything shiny.

Her hair was curled and pinned back on the sides, and she positively glowed from within. Wyatt had been worried about having the ceremony in front of cameras and the whole island, but now he knew it didn't matter.

When he was in the room with Deirdre, the whole world narrowed to just the two of them.

He walked past his mother, his brother and his family, his sister and hers, as well as a few of Deirdre's friends from her job. Norma and her husband were there, both of them sniffling, and Deirdre had invited her ex-husband and her daughter, and they both stood nearby too.

But it was really all about Wyatt and Deirdre. He reached her and drew her into a hug to a collective sigh from the guests.

There was no pastor or preacher here. He waited outside at the altar, along with the other invited guests, cameramen, and the island.

But here, Wyatt said, "Deirdre Bernard, I love you with my whole soul. I'm so glad you're going to be my wife, and that I'll get to share the rest of my life with you." He took the ring accompaniment piece he'd bought to go with her engagement ring from Scott and slipped it on her finger.

Together, they looked at the new piece, and Wyatt loved the way it curled around the larger diamond, almost making a floral arrangement.

"Wyatt Gardner," she said, twisting to get the ring from her daughter. He knew things weren't perfect between Emma and Deirdre, but he also knew they'd get better the more they worked through things. He'd only met the girl twice now, and he refused to make a judgement on her.

"I love your smile. I love how dedicated to people you are. I love how freely you love. I'm so glad we got as many chances as we did, and I can't imagine my life being as happy as it is now without you in it."

She presented him with a dark gray wedding band, with a rim of gold along both edges. "I've wanted to be your wife since the day I met you."

With the ring on his finger, Wyatt felt like everything inside his life had finally settled. Not a single piece was out of place, now that Deirdre was in his heart. He leaned down and kissed her, and he couldn't wait to establish a new normal with her as his wife.

Their closest friends and family cheered, and Wyatt hugged his brother and then his mother, ending with his sister while Deirdre embraced her daughter and her friends.

"All right," he said. "Let's go get this done." They faced the doors that led to the beach hand-in-hand, and they took the first step toward forever…together.

————

Ready for your next sweet beach romance? Read on for a sneak peek of **THE DAY HE DROVE BY**, Book 1 in the Hawthorne Harbor Romance series.

Sneak Peek! The Day He Drove By
Chapter One

1 0 years ago:

"AARON, you have to stop the car. We're not going to make it." Gretchen Samuels hated the weakness and panic in her voice, but the pain ripping through her lower back made it difficult to speak any other way.

"We're in the middle of nowhere," her husband said. "I can't stop." In fact, he accelerated to a speed their twelve-year-old sedan certainly couldn't handle.

As another labor pain tore through her, tears spilled from Gretchen's eyes. She didn't want to have her first child on the side of the road, miles from nurses and antiseptic and baby warmers. And medication. She really needed a fast-acting painkiller.

"I'm sorry," she sobbed. Aaron hated living out on her granddad's lavender farm, but the housing was cheap and he was almost done with his online securities degree. Their plans for a future in Seattle while he led the data security team at a top technology firm were months from coming to fruition.

"Don't be sorry." He glanced at her, and she disliked the panic in his eyes too, and the white-knuckle grip he had on the steering wheel certainly wasn't comforting.

Her breath caught in her throat as it seemed like this baby was going to claw its way out of her no matter how much she willed the little girl to hold on a little longer.

"Call 911," she said. "Please." She must've infused the right amount of emotion into her voice, because Aaron slowed the car and eased it onto the gravel shoulder. He leapt from behind the wheel, left his door open, and sprinted around the front of the car.

"Let's get you into the back." He supported her—the way he'd been doing for the four years they'd been together—and helped her into the backseat before pulling out his phone and making the emergency call.

Gretchen's pain eased with the new position, but it didn't go away. She wondered if it ever would, or if this degree of agony would hover in her muscles like a ghost forever. "Hang on," she whispered as she put her hand on her very pregnant belly. "Just a little while longer."

"They're on their way." Aaron poked his head back inside the car. "They said to get any blankets, towels, napkins, anything we have. You're supposed to stay lying down and try to relax."

Gretchen couldn't help the snort that escaped. "Relax?" She let her head fall back as she focused on the car's ceiling. She hadn't been able to relax for months, not since her stomach had grown so large she couldn't see her toes. Simply getting up from the couch had grown increasingly difficult as the days had passed.

She hadn't minded, because she and Aaron had wanted this baby more than anything. The tears that heated her eyes this time were from desperation. A shiver ran over her body as the wind snaked its way into the car.

"Aaron, can you close the doors?" She lifted her head but couldn't see him anywhere. Fear flowed through her. "Aaron?"

The trunk slammed, and he came to the door closest to her head this time. "We don't have a blanket in the trunk. I found this jacket though." He balled it up and put it under her head before shrugging out of the one he was wearing too.

Gretchen steeled herself to deliver her baby and wrap it in her husband's polar fleece. Her range of emotions felt ridiculous as a wave of injustice slammed into her. "Close the doors, please," she said through tight teeth. "I'm cold." Should she be cold? What if she was going into shock or something?

Her jaw worked against the rising terror as he complied, going around the car—which had all four doors open—and shutting the wind out before sealing himself behind the wheel again. Gretchen thought the silence in the car might be worse than the wind, and she didn't want to bring her baby into the world under such a cloud of awkwardness.

"Remember when we first met?" she asked him, glad when his low, soft chuckle met her ears.

"You said my hair looked like a gorilla."

She giggled too, though the motion made her stomach muscles tighten uncomfortably. She hitched in a breath and held it. Aaron had been a freshman on campus though he was twenty-three years old. Gretchen had just finished her business management degree. His dark hair was swooped to the side, very much like the cartoon gorillas Gretchen had spent a lot of time watching while she nannied to pay for school.

He reached back and threaded his fingers through hers. "What if they don't make it?" he asked, his voice barely higher than a whisper. "I don't know how to deliver a baby."

And Gretchen knew there was more than just a baby that needed to come out. "They'll make it." She spoke with as much confidence as she could, the way she always did when Aaron confessed his worries to her.

You're the best in your class, she'd tell him. You'll be able to find a good job.

Don't worry about anything here, she said to him when he had to go to Seattle to take his tests, attend interviews, or deliver dissertations. *I'll be fine. Just watching the lavender grow.*

She closed her eyes and imagined herself in the fields of lavender now, the fragrant scent of the herbs wafting through the slow, blue sky. The same smile that had always accompanied her assurances when he left drifted across her face now.

Her next labor pain stole all the peace from her, and her eyes shot open and a moan ground through her whole body. Aaron's fingers on hers squeezed, and everything seemed clenched so tight, tight, tight.

The contraction seemed to last a long time before subsiding. Gretchen only got what felt like a moment's reprieve before the next one began. Time marched on, seemingly unaware of the pain she was in, the desperate way she cinched everything tight to keep the baby inside.

She wasn't sure how many labor pains she'd endured, or how much time had gone by, before Aaron said, "They're here," with a heavy dose of relief in his voice. He once again jumped from the car.

Moments later, the door by her feet opened and a gust of ocean air raced in. The scent of brine she normally loved only reminded her that this wasn't a hospital, there were no drugs, and she could do absolutely nothing about it.

"Ma'am, my name is Andrew Herrin, and I'm going to take good care of you."

She managed to look over her belly to a man who couldn't be older than twenty. A zing of alarm raced through her.

"Drew?" She couldn't believe she cared if the man whose family lived next door to her—who she'd walked with in lavender fields as a teen—delivered her baby. He had a bag of medical supplies. A faster ride to the hospital. And a kind face, with a calm smile.

"You're going to be fine, Gretchen." He snapped a pair of gloves on and touched her ankle. "So let's see what we've got."

Sneak Peek! The Day He Drove By
Chapter Two

D rew Herrin felt the morning sun warm his back as he worked. He'd already fed the chickens, the horses, the cows, and the goats. His mother and stepfather had quite the little farm just north of Hawthorne Harbor, down the Lavender Highway. He glanced up and took a moment to just breathe, something he hadn't been able to do in Medina, though the town sat right on the water too.

The air simply tasted different here, and while Drew had hoped to make something of himself in Medina—do more, be better, actually help someone—he'd only realized the job was the same there as it was here. Just more stressful. Less fun. No room to run with his German shepherds and experiment with his ice cream flavors.

The wind picked up, but Drew was used to being windblown. Everyone on Hawthorne Harbor was. The long-time joke was that if you didn't like the wind, you should leave. Because it was always windy.

He looked across the water to the body of land he could just make out in the distance. He'd grown up on the harbor, but it still gave him a snip of surprise to remember he was looking at another country when he looked at that land.

For a fleeting moment, the same restlessness that had driven him to Medina three years ago squirreled through him again.

Then he put his head down and got back to work. He finished fixing the tractor his step-dad used to get the lavender fields properly built up for watering. He sharpened a few tools and whistled for his shepherds to come with him as he headed back to the house.

With a single bark, Blue announced his arrival from the huge flower garden adjacent to the farm. He brought the scent of roses with him, and even a white petal from a flower Drew would never know.

"You rascal." Drew grinned at the dog and flicked the petal to the ground. "You can't go over there." He glanced at the expansive garden, bearing row after row of flowers in all colors, shapes, and sizes. His family owned the land, but he'd learned that his mother rented it to a local florist in town, who apparently hand-grew everything she sold in her shop on Main Street.

Drew had never met the woman. She tended to the flowers when he wasn't there, obviously. And he had no need for flowers, as he'd sworn off women and all common dating practices when his last girlfriend had carved out his heart and then left town.

A text. That was what he'd gotten after a fifteen-month relationship where diamonds and children had been discussed.

I can't do this.

Drew thought the words his ex had sent now, though he tried to stuff all memories with Yvonne in them back into the box where he kept them.

Can't hadn't been in Drew's vocabulary growing up. His father had taught him to fix cars, tractors, lawn mowers, all of it. He worked the farm, rode horses, raised goats, planted lavender, and played a major role in the Hawthorne Harbor Lavender Festival. There was nothing Drew couldn't do.

He'd taken that attitude into adulthood, first finishing his emergency medical technician training and then going on to be a certified firefighter. He'd gone on to take cardiac life support classes, pediatric training, and tactical emergency care.

No, *can't* didn't exist in Drew's world. At least until Yvonne.

Something wet met his palm, and Drew danced away from his second German shepherd, the much more silent and sneaky Chief. A chuckle came from his throat, and Drew crouched to let his dogs lick his neck and face. His laughter grew, and he was reminded why this remote farm on the edge of Hawthorne Harbor felt more like home than anywhere else.

"Morning chores are done," he announced as he entered the wide, white farmhouse, his dogs right behind him. Their claws scratched against the hard wood, and he pointed to the utility room where he kept their food and water. "Go on, guys. I'll come let you out in a minute."

"Thanks, Drew," Joel said. His step-dad didn't mind the farm and the equipment upkeep, but his true love was with the lavender, and Drew figured they could both do what they liked best if he came out and tended to the animals.

Joel had spent the first thirty years of his life in trade carpentry, and he'd improved the inside and outside of the farmhouse until Drew barely recognized it. He stepped into the kitchen with the high, honey-colored wood beams slanting up to the vaulted ceiling to find his dark-haired mother standing at the stove.

"Morning, Ma." He swept a kiss along her hairline as she scrambled eggs. The smell made his stomach turn, and he opted for turning away and pouring himself a glass of orange juice. Funny how his father had passed nine years ago, and Drew still couldn't handle the sight and smell of his dad's favorite breakfast. How his mother continued making it every morning was a mystery to him. Thankfully, the grief that hit at unexpected times only tapped his heart today. Sometimes it could punch, leaving him breathless and confused.

"Are you working today?" she asked, switching her attention to a pan of sizzling bacon.

"Yep. Gonna shower and head in." He wondered what today would bring behind the wheel of the ambulance. Probably another cat stuck in another tree. Or a kid with a scrape or two. Drew chastised himself that he shouldn't *want* anyone in Hawthorne Harbor to need emergency medical care. But that seething need to *do something worthwhile* wouldn't seem to quiet today.

"Can I leave Blue and Chief here?"

"Yeah." Joel exhaled as he stood and refilled his coffee. "I'll take 'em out to the lavender fields and then let them swim in the harbor."

Drew smiled at the man. "Thanks, Joel. I promise I'll come get them tonight. The raccoons out here get them barking at night."

"Maybe they'll finally scare them away from my chickens," he said with a grumbly note in his voice. Joel certainly did love his fresh eggs and those clucky chickens.

"Breakfast?" his mother asked when Drew attempted to leave the kitchen.

"I'll stop at Duality on the way in." Part gas station and part eatery, the chefs at Duality made the best breakfast burritos Drew had ever tasted. He softened his rejection of her food with the biggest smile he could pull off and hooked his thumb over his shoulder. "I'm going to use the bathroom upstairs. I'll hang up my towel."

She didn't protest, and Drew took the steps two at a time to the mostly unused second floor. His old bedroom was up here, completely redone with the same luxurious hardwood Joel had gotten for next to nothing when a client decided they wanted something different. He'd painted the room in a light blue-gray and wispy white curtains had been added.

But the bedspread his mother had quilted still draped the bed, and Drew took a moment to run his fingertips along it. His favorite colors were green and blue, and he loved everything about being outside. So she'd carefully pieced together pine green pieces to make trees, dark brown pieces to make mountains, and several shades of blue to make the sky and ocean that surrounded this town Drew loved.

How he'd thought he could ever leave it and be happy plagued him. "Doesn't matter," he muttered to himself. He was back now, and happy helping around the farm as his parents got older, happy to have his old job back at the emergency services company that contracted with the hospital in Hawthorne Harbor, nearby Olympic National Park, and four other towns in the surrounding area.

After he showered, dressed, and let his dogs back outside, he climbed behind the wheel of his truck for the fifteen-minute drive into town. He loved the commute from farm to civilization. Though he didn't make it every day, the straight road and country stillness allowed his mind to wander along new flavor combinations for his ice cream fetish.

He'd been circling something new for a few days now, something he hadn't quite been able to put his taste buds on. He'd tried lavender and honey—that combination was as old as the Lavender Festival in town. White chocolate and lavender had been well-received among his paramedic teams, but he didn't think it special enough to enter the Festival's contest.

No, he definitely needed something special, something with that added oomph to make the Festival judges give him the coveted Lavender King title this year. He knew Augustus Hammond would enter the competition, and he'd won with ice cream three times out of the last six years. If Drew was going to take on the three-time Lavender King, it wasn't going to be with lavender and honey.

And he wasn't just competing against other food artisans. Oh, no. The town hosted the largest lavender festival in the entire country, and they gave out awards for revolutionary and best-use way of utilizing the plant that brought a new twist to old lavender traditions. He needed something special, but so far, it had eluded him.

He'd nearly arrived at the flavor that seemed to skip in and out of his mind when he saw a big, brown van on the side of the road up ahead. The vehicle looked older than him, and it sunk low on one corner, indicating a flat tire.

A blonde girl stood in the middle of the road, waving both of her arms. Drew immediately slowed and pulled to the gravel shoulder, giving plenty of distance between his truck and the van.

"Thank goodness." The girl ran up to his truck

before he could get fully out. She looked to be ten or eleven, with big front teeth she hadn't quite grown into yet. She had dark green eyes that had probably come half from her mother and half from her father. "You're the first car that's come along in an hour."

"Not much going on out here in the mornings," he said, glancing past her to the front driver's side, where the van leaned.

"My mom blew her tire, and we need help." The girl sized him up as if she could tell by looking alone if he could help or not. "Can you change a tire?"

"Sure I can." He gave her smile, noting that all the windows on the van were glazed dark. His defenses went up, especially because her "mom" still hadn't made an appearance. Crime was low in Hawthorne Harbor—one reason he hadn't gone to the police academy to make his certifications a trifecta in public service.

But still. This non-moving van, with all those black windows, and a little girl in the middle of the road... Drew proceeded with caution.

She played with the end of her pale ponytail. "My mom will try to tell you she can do it herself." Her voice pitched lower with every word and her eyes rounded. "But don't believe her. We've been out here for over an hour, and she's cried twice. 'The flowers,' she keeps saying." The girl turned and skipped toward the van. "Come on."

Drew took out his phone and tapped out a message to his boss. *On my way in, I ran across a motorist on the side of the road. Flat tire. Just north of mile marker seventeen on the Lavender Highway. Going to check it out.*

That way, if something happened, someone knew where he was. He'd been on the Lavender Highway hundreds of times, and he'd only stopped once—to deliver a baby almost ten years ago.

He glanced around. It had been right around here too, closer to the farm than the town, out in the middle of nowhere. He wondered what had happened to Aaron and Gretchen Samuels, and the baby girl he'd wrapped in a towel before delivering the afterbirth.

Let us know if you need help came back, and Drew pocketed his phone and shelved his memories of the last time he'd been out of a car on this stretch of the road so his senses could be on full alert.

———

Oh, something's going to happen out there on the Lavender Highway... find out what in THE DAY HE DROVE BY, Book 1 in the Hawthorne Harbor Second Chance Romance series.

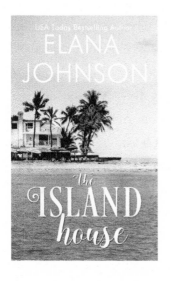

The Island House (Book 1): Charlotte Madsen's whole world came crashing down six months ago with the words, "I met someone else."

Can Charlotte navigate the healing process to find love again?

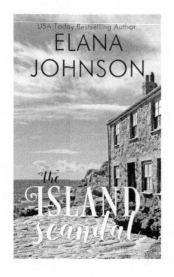

The Island Scandal (Book 2): Ashley Fox has known three things since age twelve: she was an excellent seamstress, what her wedding would look like, and that she'd never leave the island of Getaway Bay. Now, at age 35, she's been right about two of them, at least.

Can Burke and Ash find a way to navigate a romance when they've only ever been friends?

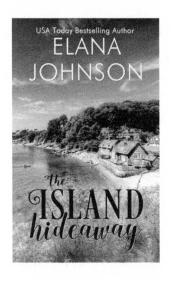

The Island Hideaway (Book 3): She's 37, single (except for the cat), and a synchronized swimmer looking to make some extra cash. Pathetic, right? She thinks so, and she's going to spend this summer housesitting a cliffside hideaway and coming up with a plan to turn her life around.

Can Noah and Zara fight their feelings for each other as easily as they trade jabs? Or will this summer shape up to be the one that provides the romance they've each always wanted?

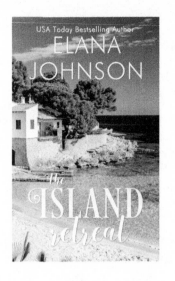

The Island Retreat (Book 4): Shannon's 35, divorced, and the highlight of her day is getting to the coffee shop before the morning rush. She tells herself that's fine, because she's got two cats and a past filled with emotional abuse. But she might be ready to heal so she can retreat into the arms of a man she's known for years...

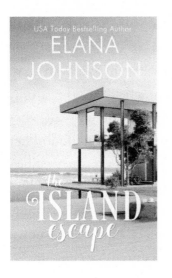

The Island Escape (Book 5): Riley Randall has spent eight years smiling at new brides, being excited for her friends as they find Mr. Right, and dating by a strict set of rules that she never breaks. But she might have to consider bending those rules ever so slightly if she wants an escape from the island...

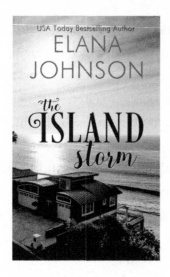

The Island Storm (Book 6): Lisa is 36, tired of the dating scene in Getaway Bay, and practically the only wedding planner at her company that hasn't found her own happy-ever-after. She's tried dating apps and blind dates...but could the company party put a man she's known for years into the spotlight?

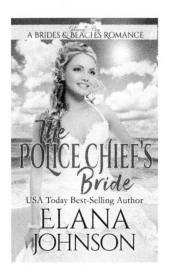

The Island Wedding (Book 7): Deirdre is almost 40, estranged from her teenaged daughter, and determined not to feel sorry for herself. She does the best she can with the cards life has dealt her and she's dreaming of another island wedding...but it certainly can't happen with the widowed Chief of Police.

Books in the Getaway Bay Resort Romance series

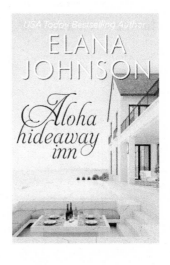

Aloha Hideaway Inn (Book 1): Can Stacey and the Aloha Hideaway Inn survive strange summer weather, the arrival of the new resort, *and* the start of a special relationship?

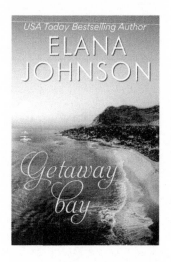

Getaway Bay (Book 2): Can Esther deal with dozens of business tasks, unhappy tourists, *and* the twists and turns in her new relationship?

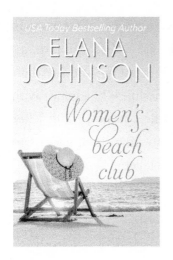

Women's Beach Club (Book 3): With the help of her friends in the Beach Club, can Tawny solve the mystery, stay safe, and keep her man?

Straw and Diamonds (Book 4): Can Sasha maintain her sanity amidst their busy schedules, her issues with men like Jasper, and her desires to take her business to the next level?

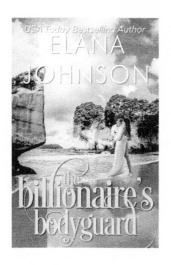

The Billionaire Club (Book 5): Can Lexie keep her business affairs in the shadows while she brings her relationship out of them? Or will she have to confess everything to her new friends...and Jason?

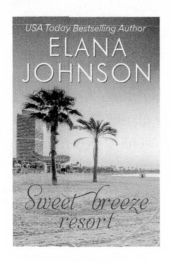

Sweet Breeze Resort (Book 6): Can Gina manage her business across the sea and finish the remodel at Sweet Breeze, all while developing a meaningful relationship with Owen and his sons?

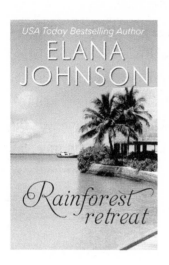

Rainforest Retreat (Book 7): As their paths continue to cross and Lawrence and Maizee spend more and more time together, will he find in her a retreat from all the family pressure? Can Maizee manage her relationship with her boss, or will she once again put her heart—and her job—on the line?

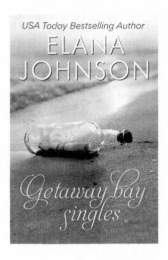

Getaway Bay Singles (Book 8): Can Katie bring him into her life, her daughter's life, and manage her business while he manages the app? Or will everything fall apart for a second time?

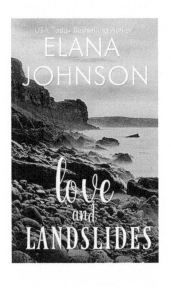

Love and Landslides (Book 1): A freak storm has her sliding down the mountain...right into the arms of her ex. As Eden and Holden spend time out in the wilds of Hawaii trying to survive, their old flame is rekindled. But with secrets and old feelings in the way, will Holden be able to take all the broken pieces of his life and put them back together in a way that makes sense? Or will he lose his heart and the reputation of his company because of a single landslide?

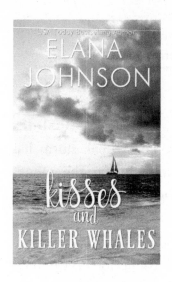

Kisses and Killer Whales (Book 2): Friends who ditch her. A pod of killer whales. A limping cruise ship. All reasons Iris finds herself stranded on an deserted island with the handsome Navy SEAL...

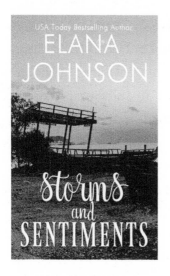

Storms and Sentiments (Book 3): He can throw a precision pass, but he's dead in the water in matters of the heart...

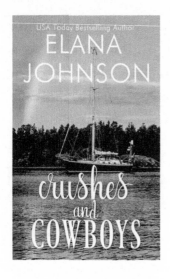

Crushes and Cowboys (Book 4): Tired of the dating scene, a cowboy billionaire puts up an Internet ad to find a woman to come out to a deserted island with him to see if they can make a love connection...

Books in the Hope Eternal Ranch Romance series

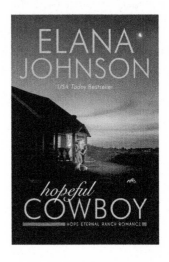

Hopeful Cowboy, Book 1: Can Ginger and Nate find their happily-ever-after, keep up their duties on the ranch, and build a family? Or will the risk be too great for them both?

Overprotective Cowboy, Book 2: Can Ted and Emma face their pasts so they can truly be ready to step into the future together? Or will everything between them fall apart once the truth comes out?

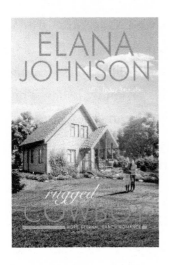

Rugged Cowboy, Book 3: He's a cowboy mechanic with two kids and an ex-wife on the run. She connects better to horses than humans. Can Dallas and Jess find their way to each other at Hope Eternal Ranch?

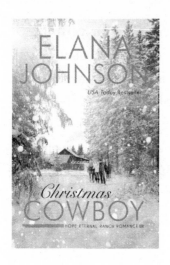

Christmas Cowboy, Book 4: He needs to start a new story for his life. She's dealing with a lot of family issues. This Christmas, can Slate and Jill find solace in each other at Hope Eternal Ranch?

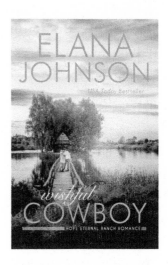

Wishful Cowboy, Book 5: He needs somewhere to belong. She has a heart as wide as the Texas sky. Can Luke and Hannah find their one true love in each other?

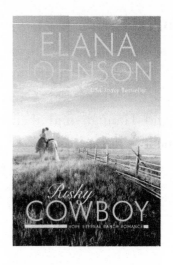

Risky Cowboy, Book 6: She's tired of making cheese and ice cream on her family's dairy farm, but when the cowboy hired to replace her turns out to be an ex-boyfriend, Clarissa suddenly isn't so sure about leaving town... Will Spencer risk it all to convince Clarissa to stay and give him a second chance?

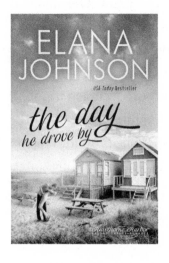

**The Day He Drove By
(Hawthorne Harbor
Second Chance Romance,
Book 1):** A widowed florist,
her ten-year-old daughter, and
the paramedic who delivered
the girl a decade earlier...

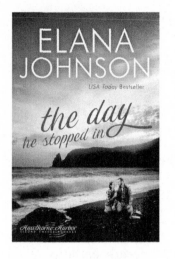

The Day He Stopped In (Hawthorne Harbor Second Chance Romance, Book 2): Janey Germaine is tired of entertaining tourists in Olympic National Park all day and trying to keep her twelve-year-old son occupied at night. When longtime friend and the Chief of Police, Adam Herrin, offers to take the boy on a ride-along one fall evening, Janey starts to see him in a different light. Do they have the courage to take their relationship out of the friend zone?

The Day He Said Hello (Hawthorne Harbor Second Chance Romance, Book 3): Bennett Patterson is content with his boring fire-fighting job and his big great dane...until he comes face-toface with his high school girlfriend, Jennie Zimmerman, who swore she'd never return to Hawthorne Harbor. Can they rekindle their old flame? Or will their opposite personalities keep them apart?

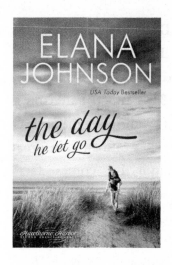

**The Day He Let Go
(Hawthorne Harbor
Second Chance Romance,
Book 4):** Trent Baker is ready
for another relationship, and
he's hopeful he can find
someone who wants him and
to be a mother to his son.
Lauren Michaels runs her own
general contract company, and
she's never thought she has a
maternal bone in her body. But when she gets a second
chance with the handsome K9 cop who blew her off
when she first came to town, she can't say no… Can
Trent and Lauren make their differences into strengths
and build a family?

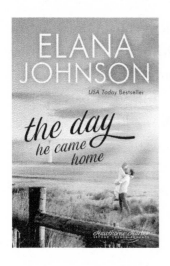

The Day He Came Home (Hawthorne Harbor Second Chance Romance, Book 5): A wounded Marine returns to Hawthorne Harbor years after the woman he was married to for exactly one week before she got an annulment...and then a baby nine months later. Can Hunter and Alice make a family out of past heartache?

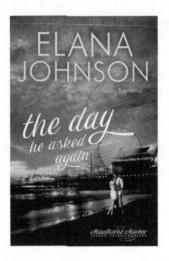

The Day He Asked Again (Hawthorne Harbor Second Chance Romance, Book 6): A Coast Guard captain would rather spend his time on the sea...unless he's with the woman he's been crushing on for months. Can Brooklynn and Dave make their second chance stick?

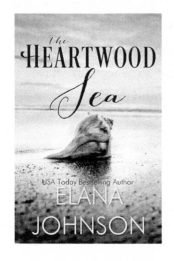

The Heartwood Sea (Book 1): She owns The Heartwood Inn. He needs the land the inn sits on to impress his boss. Neither one of them will give an inch. But will they give each other their hearts?

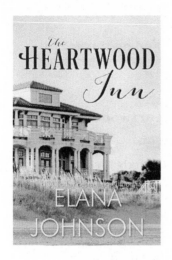

The Heartwood Inn (Book 2): She's excited to have a neighbor across the hall. He's got secrets he can never tell her. Will Olympia find a way to leave her past where it belongs so she can have a future with Chet?

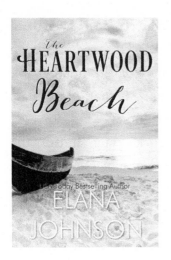

The Heartwood Beach (Book 3): She's got a stalker. He's got a loud bark. Can Sheryl tame her bodyguard into a boyfriend?

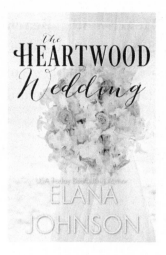

The Heartwood Wedding (Book 4): He needs a reason not to go out with a journalist. She'd like a guaranteed date for the summer. They don't get along, so keeping Brad in the not-her-real-fiancé category should be easy for Celeste. Totally easy.

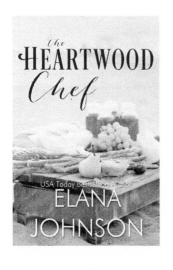

The Heartwood Chef (Book 5): They've been out before, and now they work in the same kitchen at The Heartwood Inn. Gwen isn't interested in getting anything filleted but fish, because Teagan's broken her heart before... Can Teagan and Gwen manage their professional relationship without letting feelings get in the way?

About Elana

Elana Johnson is the USA Today bestselling author of dozens of clean and wholesome contemporary romance novels. She lives in Utah, where she mothers two fur babies, taxis her daughter to theater several times a week, and eats a lot of Ferrero Rocher while writing. Find her on her website at elanajohnson.com.

Made in the USA
Monee, IL
26 June 2021

72366753R00173